You killed my father!

"Welcome, Ninja," said a voice. "I'm glad you're here. I've been starved for victims!"

Ryu turned around.

The creature that he saw was half human, half machine. Its chest muscles seemed sculpted out of metal. It held a sword in its right hand. In its left, it wielded a heavy shield that displayed the letter *J*.

"I know who you are," said Ryu. All of his Ninja training had led him to this moment. *"You killed my father!"*

**Other Worlds of Power books
you will enjoy:**

Blaster Master®
Castlevania II: Simon's Quest®
Metal Gear®
Wizards & Warriors®

NINJA GAIDEN®

A novel based on the best-selling game
by TECMO®

Book created by F.X. Nine
Written by A.L. Singer
A Seth Godin Production

**This book is not authorized, sponsored, or endorsed
by Nintendo of America Inc.**

SCHOLASTIC INC.
New York Toronto London Auckland Sydney

Special thanks to: Greg Holch, Jean Feiwel, Dick Krinsley, Dona Smith, Amy Berkower, Sheila Callahan, Nancy Smith, Joan Giurdanella, and especially Robert Leitgeb, Kevin Blackburn and Dimitri Criona.

ISBN 0-590-43776-3

12 11 10 9 8 7 6 5 4 3   0 1 2 3/9

Printed in the U.S.A   01

First Scholastic printing, July 1990

*This book is dedicated to the Ninja
in everyone's dad.*

CHAPTER 1

The blindfold was tight. Very tight. In the back, it pulled on Ryu Hayabusa's hair.

He waited for his attacker. His steel-gray eyes were wide open, meeting nothing but solid blackness.

But Ryu Hayabusa saw everything.

Not with his eyes. They were only one sense, one of six. And if you only trusted one sense, you were dead.

Ryu heard a flutter above him. Instantly he knew what is was: A red-winged blackbird. Leaving a Japanese red maple tree. Flying south-southwest.

His ears told him that. The smell of the bark. The slight shifting of the breeze against his skin.

No ordinary person could put all this information together without seeing.

To a Ninja, it was a way of life.

He took three steps and stopped. His opponent was coming.

Ryu's body loosened, relaxed. That was

the Ninja way. Let the other attack first; use his energy against him.

Footsteps. From the left.

Height. About six feet one, five inches taller than Ryu.

The punch. From the right, about chest high.

Whooosh.

Ryu stepped aside — his *yoko-aruki* step was perfect.

The punch sailed past. Then another followed.

Instantly Ryu's right hand shot out. He made contact, hitting the outside of his attacker's arm.

"Yaaaagh!" came the cry of pain.

Ryu raised his leg and planted the sole of his *tabi* boot squarely on his rival's hip.

One down.

He whirled around. There was another one coming.

A sword? Ryu sensed it, but could it possibly be true? Fear bolted through him — for a split second.

The swordsman planted his feet. He thrust quickly, but Ryu leapt to the side.

Ryu landed and punched his opponent's sword hand. In one fluid motion he leaned in, grabbed both of the other man's hands, and twisted the arms upward.

Stepping behind the swordsman's leg, Ryu threw him to the ground.

"Ooof!" the man cried out, landing with a heavy *thud*.

Ryu stood upright again. He balanced his weight, let his arms go slack. He was prepared for his next challenge.

Instead, he heard voices. Mumbling voices. He knew who the voices belonged to, and he knew they were not going to attack him. Ryu was safe.

But he was scared. For the first time in all his thirteen years, he felt fear racing through him. Ryu, who could laugh in the face of a knife-wielding marauder. Ryu, who wouldn't flinch if a samurai were to suddenly rise from the dead and charge at him.

These voices were making Ryu shake in his shoes. And when one of them boomed loudly, he couldn't keep himself from jumping.

"You may remove your blindfold, Ryu Hayabusa," the voice said.

Ryu did as he was told. A few yards away, three black-belt Ninja instructors stood near a gingko tree. The one in the middle, Akira, had been his mentor since birth. Now Akira was staring at him.

Ryu tried to swallow, but his throat was too dry. He felt as if a flock of Japanese butterflies had just broken out of cocoons in his stomach. With a weak smile, he asked, "Did I do it?"

Akira walked over to him, slowly. His

face was grim and concentrated, and he averted Ryu's eyes.

Panic gripped Ryu. What had gone wrong?

Akira stopped two feet before his prize pupil. He grabbed Ryu's shoulder firmly. And before he spoke, his eyes betrayed a glimmer — of what? Fury? Mockery? Mischief? Happiness? Ryu couldn't tell.

"Ryu," Akira said softly. "Congratulations. You have achieved your *dan* grade. From this day on, you are the highest class of Ninja warrior . . . and the best I have ever seen in my life."

Ryu tried to keep calm. He wanted to thank Akira humbly. He wanted to say that it was Akira, not he, who deserved the praise. But when he opened his mouth, only one word came out:

"YAAAAAHHH-HOOOOOOOOO!"

GAME HINT

To beat the Barbarian, throw small *shuriken*, then hit him with your sword.

CHAPTER 2

"Ryu, darling, I'm so happy for you." Mrs. Hayabusa's dark eyes glowed with warmth. She returned her son's enthusiastic hug, and realized once again that she had to stand on tiptoe. Her boy had grown so much.

Ryu tore himself away. "I don't believe it! No, I do believe it! I don't know what I believe! Oh, this is incredible!" He let out a whoop of joy and leapt into the air.

Mrs. Hayabusa laughed. "I have never seen you like this, my son."

"I've never *felt* like this!" For the first time since coming home, he set down the small box he had been carrying. Opening it delicately, he pulled out the only item of clothing he had ever cared about.

His black belt.

He tried it on and felt power surging through him. "How does it look, Mom?"

Mrs. Hayabusa looked deeply into her son's eyes. "Beautiful, Ryu," she said, her voice barely above a whisper. "Just . . . beautiful."

Ryu nodded. His joy had overwhelmed him. He had hardly been able to see straight. But his mother's eyes brought him back to earth. There was sadness behind them, and Ryu knew why.

"It's time, I guess, huh?" he said.

Ryu could tell his mother was trying not to look upset. She held her head high and smiled. "My dearest son," she said, "I know your fate was determined for you many, many years ago. You began your training when you were still in diapers. I have watched you, seen your progress, shared your joy. And I know that all of it was in preparation for this day. But somehow . . . "

Her voice broke. Ryu rushed to her side and put his arm around her.

She let him stay there a moment, taking comfort silently. Then she gently took his arm away and walked across the living room. The delicate straw tatami mat rustled under her footsteps. She stopped at the oaken chest and choked back a sob. Pulling open the top drawer, she took out a sealed envelope.

Holding it in her trembling fingers, she turned to face her son. "When your father left Tokyo for America, he was a young man," she began. "He was so proud of his newborn baby boy, Ryu. He couldn't wait to come home from his expedition, and neither could I. I remember his parting words exactly: 'I give you this, my dear Asami, with a reluctant heart. I know I will be seeing you within two weeks, but in the unlikely event I should not return, save this letter, this *gaiden*, until little Ryu has become a man. On that day, you must give it to him and wish him success with all your heart.' "

Ryu nodded. He had heard the story as a little boy and never forgotten it.

"I was startled," Mrs. Hayabusa continued, "but your father comforted me. He assured me he would come home, and I believed him." She lowered her eyes. "Never did I think I would have to give this to you, Ryu."

A tear rolled down her cheek as she handed her son the envelope.

Ryu took it. He felt icy cold, numb. He was torn between the urge to comfort his mother and the call of destiny that had driven him every day of his life.

The envelope was yellowed with age. He shuddered when he saw the words written on it: FOR RYU UPON HIS PASSAGE TO MANHOOD. His father's faded handwriting was an eerie reminder of the man he had never met — the man whose disappearance he still did not understand . . .

CHAPTER 3

Thirteen years earlier, the world had been different. Some say it was a kinder and slower place. Others say it was harsh and cruel. To Dr. Ken Hayabusa, an American-born Japanese archaeologist, it was simply the most exciting time to be alive. His wife had given birth to a handsome, healthy son, and he had finally begun the expedition of his career. The one that was sure to win him worldwide recognition in his field. He was beyond happy. He awoke each day practically exploding with joy. Although he knew his trek might be dangerous, he had taken all the necessary precautions.

How could he have known that his precautions were in vain? How could he have possibly known the bizarre fate that awaited him?

"Randolph, you are a wimp!"

Ken Hayabusa bounded through the dense brush of the Amazon jungle. Overhead, the noon sun was a fireball that seemed to lick his skin with its flames. The humidity clung to him, tropical insects hovered in thick swarms around his face, and low-hanging branches whipped him at every turn. But he barely noticed any of it.

They were almost there.

He paused a moment, adjusted his backpack and sword belt. He remembered how his colleagues had laughed when he insisted on taking the sword. No matter. Not even the most up-to-date ammunition made him feel as safe as his sword. It was an old and trusted friend. And in times of need, friends never let you down.

"Randolph?" he called out again. "Have I lost you, old fellow?"

Several yards behind him, an overweight, bearded man stumbled through a greenish-yellow thicket. He crashed to the ground, sending the contents of his backpack sprawling.

"I don't know why I ever agreed to go along with this crack-brained scheme," he mumbled.

Dr. Hayabusa sprinted over to help him up. "For the pursuit of knowledge, my friend!" he said with a laugh. "Surely this can't be the Doctor Randolph Wimple, shining star of the University of Peru archaeology department!"

"Spare me the guilt trip, Ken," Dr. Wimple replied. "Can't we just sit for a minute? You may be a black-belt Ninja, my friend, but I'm an ordinary human. The ruins have been there for hundreds of years. They'll be exactly the same, whether we get there now or five hours from now."

"Yes, but my son is changing by the minute!" Dr. Hayabusa said, pacing anxiously. "I can't wait to return to my family with the news of our great success, Randolph!"

Dr. Wimple sighed. "Just my luck to get stuck with a romantic sap. All right, if we must hurry, so be it. Just be careful — you know the dangers."

Of course he did. Every archaeologist knew them. Of the twenty-nine explorers who had tried to reach the ruins, none had ever returned. No bodies had ever been found.

No one knew what was inside the ruins. There were rumors of dragons and monsters, but those were never taken seriously. One thing was clear though — whatever was there must be of great historical importance. And awesome power.

"Demons, eh, Randolph?" Dr. Hayabusa chuckled. "You're afraid some drooling, fire-breathing monster is going to gobble us down — is that it?"

"Well, no. I was just saying that — "

"Don't forget, Randolph. This is the late twentieth century." He resumed his pacing.

"None of the other explorers had the sophisticated tracking devices we have, the weaponry, the communications setup — "

"Yes, and space-age technology like your sword," Dr. Wimple said dryly.

"A cheap shot, Randolph! You know that — "

Before he could say another word, Dr. Hayabusa disappeared into the ground.

"Ken!" Dr. Wimple exclaimed. He rushed to the hole where his colleague had been standing.

"Randolph?" came a muffled voice from within the hole. "What do you suppose a bear trap would be doing in the middle of a tropical jungle?"

Dr. Wimple put his hand to his mouth. "Oh, dear!" He reached down and pulled his colleague out. "Were you — "

"Caught in it?" Dr. Hayabusa said, dusting himself off. "No. I was saved by several decades of rust. The trap couldn't close."

"Well, I suppose we must be getting near our site," Dr. Wimple said. "Someone is trying to protect it."

"*Was* trying to protect it, Randolph," Dr. Hayabusa corrected. "Judging from that trap, it looks as if they may have given up years ago."

"Lucky for us, I suppose."

"You see?" Dr. Hayabusa said, heading

back into the woods. "We have nothing to fear — "

"GRRRRRAAAAGGGGHHHH!"

Dr. Hayabusa swallowed his last word. There was a lizard in his path. But this was not a cute little slithery pest.

It was six feet long and angry. And its enormous teeth glinted in the sun as they lunged at Dr. Hayabusa's face!

CHAPTER 4

Dr. Hayabusa leapt out of the monster's path. He fell to the ground.

Scrambling to his feet, he unsheathed his sword.

The beast stared at him. Its eyes rolled about on either side of its face. Its short, stocky legs stuck out the side of its scaly body and curved down, like a person at the top of a pushup. Slowly it approached, letting out a fearsome hiss.

"Spear it, Ken!" Dr. Wimple cried out.

Dr. Hayabusa walked backward. He held his sword steady. "Come this way, Randolph! Walk slowly. It won't harm us. It needs to conserve its energy."

Dr. Wimple obeyed. "How can you possibly know that?"

"The creature is a Komodo dragon, Randolph. Until now it has only been found on the Indonesian island of Komodo, having somehow survived extinction. As a cold-blooded reptile, it often sleeps in the sunlight, replenishing its energy. You can see this one is a bit sluggish. At night, it will undoubtedly be quick and ferocious."

"Th-thank you," Dr. Wimple said, trembling. "I sh-shall make sure not to be around here after dark."

"But what a zoological find! The first of its kind discovered in the West!"

Dr. Wimple nodded. "Fine. We'll write a report. Now let's get out of here before we become its lunch!"

They took off, scampering deeper into the jungle. The trees grew closer together, the brush thicker and thornier. Dr. Hayabusa used his sword to cut a path.

They bushwhacked for hours. Under the afternoon sun, the jungle festered. The humidity practically suffocated them, and they had to stop every few feet to catch their breaths. Even Dr. Hayabusa was running out of steam.

When they reached a clearing, Dr. Wimple flopped onto the ground. "Siesta time," he said. "I don't care what you say."

Dr. Hayabusa took a map out of his pocket. He studied it carefully. "If I'm not mistaken, Randolph, we are already at the — "

"Ken! Look!" Dr. Wimple shouted. Suddenly his fatigue disappeared. He ran across the clearing, to a strange, rounded stone that stuck out of the ground.

Pulling a spade out of his backpack, Dr. Wimple furiously dug around the stone. It was a large, flat tablet, covered with intricate etchings.

Dr. Hayabusa joined his colleague, and together they pulled out the tablet. They set it down, and Dr. Hayabusa began to translate:

"All praise the Great Hero Shinobi, who, on this day in Anno Domini 1290, confronted the powerful Demon of the Temple of Darkness."

"Shinobi?" Dr. Wimple interrupted. "That's impossible! How could a Japanese be in the Amazon, two hundred years before Columbus?"

His eyes aglow, Dr. Hayabusa read on:

"Having sailed across the Eternal Sea to find the Land of Forbidden Mystery, Shinobi returned to his native land, guarding the secret of his discovery."

"Eureka!" Dr. Wimple shouted. "Do you realize what a find we've made? My associates can carbon-date it to make sure it's not a fake, and — "

"The Great Shinobi cannot bear to re-

veal the one shame of his life," Dr. Hayabusa continued reading,

> *" . . . his only failure as a warrior. When the Demon's body lay bloodless on the ground, slain by Shinobi's sword, its power lived on. It continued the fight, unleashing the forces of nature. Though Shinobi could not beat this invisible enemy, he fought bravely, dividing the Demon's energy in two — the forces of Light and Dark.*
> *Thus disabling the Demon, he imprisoned the forces into two statues, buried hereunder."*

Without saying another word, the two scientists dropped to their knees and began digging. It took over an hour, but when their shovels hit two solid objects, they were delirious with excitement.

Dr. Hayabusa pulled out a white marble figurine, about a foot tall and shaped like a horrible, hunched dragon. Dr. Wimple's statue was exactly the same, except made of black onyx.

"Remarkable!" Dr. Wimple said in an awed whisper. "Does the tablet explain what happened to their power?"

Dr. Hayabusa picked up the tablet and read more:

"The Demon will begin to wake at the time of the Dark Moon, approximately every 700 years. If the statues are in the same temple as the Demon, they will join forces and inhabit the Demon's body, releasing unimaginable power. The world will not survive. However, if the statues are not inside the temple, the Demon will remain harmless."

Dr. Hayabusa paused. His face was solemn.

"Is that it?" Dr. Wimple asked.

"Yes." Dr. Hayabusa looked his friend in the eye. "The question is, where is the temple?"

Dr. Wimple threw back his head in laughter. "Surely you don't take all that seriously?"

"What do you mean? We did find the statues."

"Yes, and they're fine examples of pre-Columbian South American art. But it's obvious what happened here. Clearly Shinobi's Demon was a Komodo dragon, an ancestor of the one we found! The rest, the pagan mumbo jumbo, we should leave to the folklore experts!"

Dr. Wimple took off his pack and stuffed the statues in. Then he walked into the surrounding jungle, snooping around.

But Dr. Hayabusa wasn't convinced. He paced the edge of the clearing, trying to piece it all together.

His toe stubbed against the edge of another stone. Gritting his teeth, he looked down at it. It was gold, and it looked like the edge of something bigger.

He knelt down and yanked the underbrush off its surface. When he was done, a small, perfectly square stone stared up at him. On it were gold inlays, depicting some kind of message. "Amazing," he called out. "I've found an ancient grave marker, Randolph!"

No answer. Dr. Hayabusa turned around. "Randolph?" He walked across the clearing, looking around. "Randolph, where did you go?"

Creeeeeak.

He stopped. That wasn't a jungle sound. Randolph Wimple must have found something else in the woods. But where? In the thick air, it was hard to tell where the noise came from.

Creeeeeak.

He felt his blood freeze. The sound was in the clearing, behind him.

He whipped around. Everything looked exactly the same. Or did it?

Creeeeeak.

It was the grave marker. His trained eyes detected a slight movement. An inner voice told him — begged him — to run away.

But Dr. Hayabusa walked closer.

Shcrrraaawwwwwwwwwk — clunk!

The marker slid aside, revealing a deep hole.

And two arms.

A sudden, blinding lightning bolt ripped the jungle air. It flashed in front of Dr. Hayabusa and sliced a nearby tree in half. Dr. Hayabusa flung himself on the ground.

When he turned around, his jaw dropped open.

Standing in front of him was a creature. It was human, but only barely. Each foot had three enormous claws. Its bare chest rippled with muscles that looked like cast iron. Deadly sharp ram horns jutted out of the steel mask that covered its face. In its right hand, it held a sword. In its left, a gleaming shield emblazoned with the letter *J*.

And when it spoke, the ground shook.

"Give me the statues!" it demanded.

"Not on your life, sheep face!" Dr. Hayabusa said.

The warrior thrust the sword. Its mighty stroke caused the trees to rustle.

With a perfect Ninja front roll, Dr. Hayabusa escaped the sword. He sprang to his feet. In one swift motion, he pulled his own sword and lunged.

CLANNNNNNG! It hit against his enemy's shield. Dr. Hayabusa stepped back, waiting for the next move.

The warrior dropped its sword. With a casual but powerful gesture, it reached upward. Dr. Hayabusa watched with eagle eyes.

Craaaaaaack! Another bolt of lightning sliced the sky. This one connected with the warrior's outstretched hand.

Dr. Hayabusa stared in disbelief. How could this *thing* have survived the hit?

It brought its arm forward. It pointed. *DZZZZZZZZIT!*

"*Yeeaaaaaagh!*" Dr. Hayabusa took the full force of the electric current. He crumbled to the ground.

"A freak storm!" came a voice from behind him. "Well, maybe there'll be a break in the humidity — "

Out of the corner of his eye, Dr. Hayabusa saw Randolph Wimple emerge from the surrounding brush.

He propped himself on weakened elbows. "Run!" he croaked, his voice raw.

Dr. Wimple froze in his tracks. He looked from Dr. Hayabusa to the warrior. "Ken! Who — what — "

"Run for your life!" Dr. Hayabusa croaked. "And follow every step of Emergency Plan F! Do you understand?"

"But — but I can't just leave you — " Dr. Wimple was cut off by another electric jolt. It drilled a clean hole through the tree next to him.

Dr. Wimple was off in a flash. He had never run so fast in his life.

"Good riddance," the warrior snarled. **"Now give me the statues."**

"Never!" Dr. Hayabusa said, stalling. By now, Dr. Wimple would be fifty yards away.

With both statues.

DZZZZIT! Another jolt made Dr. Hayabusa arch in pain. "All right!" he said. "At least leave me with enough strength to open my pack."

The warrior waited. With agonized slowness, Dr. Hayabusa removed his backpack. The longer he took, the farther Dr. Wimple would travel. He set the pack down. He fumbled with the laces. He removed his canteen from the top. He dumped the contents on the ground.

Trail mix, three maps, a wallet, a camera, two lenses, a mess kit, and a compass. Nothing more.

The warrior seemed to swell with rage. Veins strained at its chest muscles. With its fists clenched, it reached up to the sky. A deafening boom shook the entire jungle. The lightning that struck the warrior's hand bathed the area in white light. When the flash was over, the warrior glowed.

"No one plays games with me, foolish insect," it bellowed. "Prepare to meet a fate more unimaginably terrible than death!"

> ## GAME HINT
> To beat Kelbeross, get under the left podium, and hit him with your windmill star when he's coming from the right. Then (staying under the podium), hit the other Kelbeross with your sword or your star.

CHAPTER 5

Randolph Wimple was sick with guilt. But that wasn't all. He limped from a twisted ankle. His pants were ripped from a thorny bush, his hair matted with sweat. From head to toe, he was covered with dirt. As he stumbled into the hotel at the edge of the jungle, people avoided him.

The hotel lobby was stuffy and hot. A worker stood on a high ladder in the center, replacing a light bulb on a ceiling fan that wasn't working.

I left him to die. That was the only thought running through Dr. Wimple's head. It repeated itself over and over again. He didn't know how he could live with it.

Hobbling across the lobby, he reached a bank of telephone booths. He tried to enter one, but his backpack wouldn't fit. He took the pack off and put it on the floor, making sure to wrap the shoulder harnesses around his ankle. Just in case.

"Plan F," he muttered, fumbling in his pocket for change. "What was Plan F?"

His fingers shook as he deposited his

coins in the phone. It seemed to take forever, but his secretary finally answered. "Ellie? Wimple here. Listen closely, you've got to send — what? No, Ellie, I *won't* be making the faculty seminar on Monday. I don't even know if I'll be *alive* on Monday — "

A twinge of pain shot up his leg. Must be the twisted ankle, he assumed. He shifted his weight to the other foot. He looked down to check the backpack.

It was gone.

There was a clattering of footsteps across the lobby's linoleum floor. Two men in white shirts were running away. One of them held the pack.

Dr. Wimple dropped the phone receiver. He raced across the lobby. His exhaustion was gone, and he could barely feel his feet touch the ground.

It took about five steps for his ankle to give out.

"Yiiaaaa!" Dr. Wimple flailed his arms, grabbing the ladder for support. At the top, the worker windmilled his arms, trying to keep his balance. A light bulb flew out of his hand.

Pockkkk! The bulb exploded on the floor, sounding like a pistol shot.

Startled, the two thugs jumped. They dove to the floor.

At the same time, Dr. Wimple collapsed

in pain. He landed in a heap, his out-stretched arms inches from the backpack.

The thugs lunged. Dr. Wimple grabbed.

"Give...me...that..." Dr. Wimple said, desperately clinging to his pack.

The thugs ripped open the top. One of them reached inside, the other pushed Dr. Wimple.

But not before Dr. Wimple had his hands inside the pack. His fingers closed around something smooth and heavy. He hoped it was a statue.

"Nnngaaaah!" cried one of the thugs, shoving Dr. Wimple violently.

Dr. Wimple rolled away, pulling out whatever was in his hands. When he stood up, he saw the two thieves scrambling out the doorway with the backpack.

He felt his arms being grabbed. "All right, you bum, you're out of here!" came a gruff voice.

Dr. Wimple looked to his right and left, into the stern faces of two hotel security guards. "Pardon me, senors," he said, "but you have the wrong man — "

That was all he could say before they tossed him out the front door. He cried out in excruciating pain as he landed on the well-trampled dirt out front.

When the first wave of pain settled

down, he looked at his hand.

He was gripping so tight that his knuckles were white. As white as the object he was holding.

The Light statue.

It had been the worst day of Dr. Wimple's life. He had abandoned his colleague, broken his ankle, been humiliated by hotel guards, and allowed two common criminals to steal one of the most valuable relics known to man.

But he had one small satisfaction. The two statues were separate. They could never end up in the temple together.

Not that he really *believed* the ancient inscription.

But you never know.

CHAPTER 6

My beloved son,
   I haven't left home yet and already
I miss you with all my heart.

Ryu felt a knot in his throat as he began to read. His whole life he had dreamed of meeting his dad, imagined what he would look like, what he'd say. Now his dad's own words were staring at him, talking to him. Like a conversation, after all these years!

Half a conversation, really. Ryu longed to answer. *I miss you, too!* he would say. Then he would fill his dad in on thirteen years. There was so much to tell. His dad would barely get a word in edgewise.

He sighed. All he could do was read, imagine, dream. It was better than nothing.

Each day away from you I will always regret, and when I race home in two weeks, your poor mother will not be able to tear you out of my arms. Then, I will rip this letter up. You will never be able to read it and laugh at my sentimental feelings when you are a teenager. If you are reading this, my son, it means that I did not return. It means that you are now at the end of your training, and you are ready to complete the mission I have failed.

Ryu, when I leave for South America, I will take my second most-trusted sword. I leave the first, the Dragon Sword, for you. It makes me laugh to imagine your tiny fingers around it now, but I know someday you will become a Ninja, finer and braver than I. Take this sword to America, and look for Dr. Walter Smith, a renowned archaeologist. He will tell you what happened, and what to do.

Be always on your guard, and never forget the last words of the ancient poem I whispered in your ear before I left:

"And when you're lost, my son,
When joy becomes despair,
I'll send a star of deepest gold,
To let you know I'm there."

Your loving father

Ryu put down the letter. He looked into his mother's red-tinged eyes. She wanted to ask about the letter. But she didn't.

"You're leaving, aren't you?" were her only words.

"Yes, Mom," Ryu answered. She started to shake, and Ryu took her hand gently. They sat down on the tatami mat. "I am leaving. But I promise I'll return. And if I find whoever it was that killed Dad, he will regret the day he was born."

Mrs. Hayabusa sniffled, then nodded. The silence hung in the air. He could tell she wanted to believe but couldn't quite bring herself to.

"I promise," he repeated.

Before the words left his mouth, he knew how hollow they sounded. He knew he had a hard time believing them himself.

GAME HINT

To beat Basequr, use the windmill star and throw it at his bullets. When it returns to you, jump over it and it will hit him.

CHAPTER 7

Ryu looked up at the sign above the wrought-iron gate: GALESBURG UNIVERSITY.

This was the place. Galesburg, New Mexico. Home of Dr. Walter Smith.

It had been a long trip. After reading his father's letter, Ryu had taken the first flight from Tokyo to Los Angeles. At the airport, he had spent two solid hours at a pay phone tracking down Dr. Smith's address. The bus ride from L.A. to Galesburg had felt as if it would go on forever.

Now, finally, he was here.

He stepped through the gate. Seeing the fresh-mowed lawn, surrounded by ivy-covered buildings, he could barely control his excitement. Would Dr. Smith know about his father? Would he know what had happened to him? Was he —

Suddenly Ryu was jerked backward.

"Where do you think you're going, pal?"

Ryu looked up. The voice belonged to a campus security guard. There was one on either side of him, gripping the sleeves of his solid black Ninja uniform.

"To see Doctor Smith," Ryu replied calmly.

"A nut," the other guard said to his partner. "They get younger all the time."

"I hope that thing is rubber," the other one said. "Otherwise, you're in big trouble."

The sword. That's what they were looking at. Ryu laughed. "No, no, you don't understand. This is an ancient Ninja weapon. I'm not going to use it . . . it's for Doctor Smith's archaeology project. Go ahead and call him; tell him Ryu Hayabusa is here. He'll let me in."

The guards exchanged an uneasy glance. "Look, kid," the first one said, "I don't care if you're Bruce Lee. No weapons on campus."

"Besides," the second one added, "he isn't here."

"Where is he?" Ryu asked.

"None of your business."

Ryu could have created a scene. He could have battled the guards and won easily. But in a situation like this, it was best to use your head.

Nodding politely to the guards, Ryu turned away. He checked his watch, which read one-fifteen. If Dr. Smith really wasn't on campus, chances were he'd be having lunch somewhere.

He walked a short distance to the center of Galesburg. Its main street had a few small stores, a bus stop, and a car wash. At the end of the street, separated from the car wash by a narrow alleyway, was a restaurant called Jay's.

Rock music throbbed from the windows of Jay's. It didn't seem like the place for a distinguished professor, but you never knew. When Ryu walked in, he felt bombarded by sound. Almost every table was full of people, laughing and talking as loud as they could. At the bar there was a rowdy crowd, about two deep.

Ryu walked up to a waitress who was filling out a check at the bar. "Excuse me," he said. "Have you seen Doctor Walter Smith here? He's a professor at the university."

"You just missed him," she replied. "Left for the parking lot a minute ago."

"Thank you very much," Ryu said.

"Thank you very much," a voice mimicked to his right. It was high-pitched, singsong, mocking.

Ryu ignored it and turned away.

"*Love* your sword," the voice added. "Did you save up a lot of box tops to get it?"

There was a roar of laughter from the bar. Ryu turned around. Leering at him from under a red baseball cap was a tall, broad-shouldered guy with a toothpick in his mouth. About 200 pounds, Ryu estimated. Weight lifter. In his twenties.

"Excuse me?" Ryu said.

"You're excused," the guy said. He removed the toothpick from his mouth. "But first, I challenge you to a duel."

He lunged at Ryu, using the toothpick as a sword. Ryu stepped aside. His reflexes went to work. When his attacker's arm was fully extended, Ryu pushed it sharply. At the same time, he stuck his leg in the man's path. With a grunt of surprise and pain, the attacker fell to the floor.

There was a sudden hush at the bar. "Flatten the dude, Bonzo!" someone called out.

"Take it outside, fellas!" the bartender warned.

Springing to his feet, Bonzo was flushed with anger. "I'll be happy to take it outside," he said through clenched teeth. "If this wimp will come with me."

Ryu nodded. "If that's what you want."

"But you have to put away your toy."

"If you mean my sword," Ryu said, "I would be happy to face you without it."

Bonzo rolled up the sleeves of his flannel shirt. "Okay, buddy, let's go." He began walking to the door.

Instantly, five muscular men rose from their stools at the bar. Ryu felt as if he were facing the front line of the Dallas Cowboys.

He followed Bonzo outside and into the alleyway beside the building. The others clomped behind him.

Scraps of food and paper littered the alley. Three small animals scurried under a hulking old Dumpster. When Ryu stopped, he was surrounded by the men. In the shadow of the restaurant, they were dark and faceless.

"Sword off," Bonzo demanded.

Ryu looked around calmly. "I thought this was going to be a fair fight." He began unhooking his belt. "But I learned long ago that fighting a gang of cowards is much easier than fighting one honest opponent."

Bonzo's body tensed with fury. "That does it! Get him, boys!"

At once, they all jumped toward Ryu, fists flying. Ryu fell to the ground and rolled away, still clutching his sword. He came to his feet in the clear, several yards away. He was close to the alley entrance. If he wanted to, he could have run away.

Instead, he faced his bewildered attackers and said, "What would your coach say about that move?"

Snarling, they ran toward him.

"Stop!" a voice suddenly shouted from behind Ryu.

The men all obeyed. Their eyes were wide with shock.

Ryu spun around. He came face-to-face with a beautiful young woman, not much older than he was.

It wasn't her the men were shocked to see. It was the pistol in her hand.

Pointed at Ryu.

Ryu was a Ninja, but even a Ninja wasn't invulnerable. And he didn't even have time to think before she shot him point-blank.

CHAPTER 8

White light.

Above him. To the side of him. Below him. Everything was white.

Something passed in front of him. He could tell by the slight shift in the room's air, by the gradation of darkness that went slowly by. After all, a Ninja was a Ninja, alive or —

Ryu couldn't finish the sentence, even in his thoughts.

He struggled to open his eyes but couldn't. He tried to move his hands but they were locked. When he attempted to speak, his mouth wouldn't budge.

Whatever was in the room moved. It was coming closer to him. It had a voice.

"Ryu."

The white light moved and flickered. Ryu saw a sharp outline, a light fixture. Then nothing. He realized his eyelids were fluttering.

"Ryu Hayabusa, if you can hear me, nod your head."

Ryu felt waves of pain and nausea as

he tried to obey. "Ohhhhh," he managed to groan.

He was alive — and he still had his sword. He could feel it by his side. Slowly he sat up.

He was in a small white room with a fluorescent light above. There were no windows, just an air-conditioning vent.

The girl was standing before him. The one who had shot him. She waited patiently for his eyes to settle on her. Then she thrust a small, heavy sack into his right hand.

"Take this," she said. "Don't ask any questions. Just run!"

"But—who are—" Ryu began to ask.

"If you want to live, then go now!" she said, cutting him off.

Her tone of voice meant business. Clutching the sack, Ryu ran out the door.

His footsteps clattered against the metal floor of a long, dark hallway. He breathed stale, musty air. In the distance he could hear a shrill siren. Probably an alarm.

He wound his way through a maze of hallways. At the end of one, there was a long stairway leading upward. At the bottom step, he looked over his shoulder. No one was following.

He was in luck. He sprinted up the stairs to a heavy steel door. Pushing it open, he stepped outside.

The door opened in the back of a tiny cave. Surrounded by total darkness, Ryu felt his way along the craggy walls.

When he got to the cave opening, he walked out into the sun-baked New Mexico desert. The cave was in the side of a long, flat mesa. About a mile to his right, the town of Galesburg lay at the foothills of the Sandia Mountains.

Ryu ran toward the town. When he was sure no one was following him, he opened the sack he'd been given.

Inside was a small statue made of some black substance that looked like marble. It had the shape of a dragon, hunched and snarling. Probably some smuggled sculpture, he thought. He decided to hold on to it. After he saw Dr. Smith, he could take it to a police station.

This time, when he got to the University gate, the guards weren't so unfriendly.

"What did you say your name was?" the first one asked.

"Ryu Hayabusa," Ryu answered.

"That's what Doctor Smith said," the other one interjected.

"He mentioned my name?" Ryu asked, confused.

"I told him some kid came, with some kind of Japanese-sounding name," the first one replied. "I tried to remember it, got as far as Haya — "

"His eyes lit up like a Christmas tree," the second one added with a smile. "I guess he knows you. Go on in, first building to your left, room 217."

"Thanks!" Ryu ran across the quadrangle and into the building. He knocked on the door to room 217, then turned the knob and entered.

The first things he noticed were the maps. Dozens of them, plastered on the walls, strewn over all the surfaces. There were floor-to-ceiling bookshelves on each wall, stacked with papers, magazines, tapes, books.

And in the center of it all was a rumpled old man with a thick white beard and a potbelly. His piercing eyes stared through thick wire-rimmed glasses. He seemed to be examining Ryu, as if for an interrogation.

But when he spoke, his voice was soft, almost tender. "You look . . . just like your father," was all he said.

Ryu walked up to the desk. "You knew him, didn't you?" he said. "You know what happened to him!"

"Please, sit," Dr. Smith said, gesturing to a chair.

"I can't." Emotions were coursing through Ryu like electric connections. He wanted to jump with joy, he wanted to ask Dr. Smith a thousand questions at the same time. The last thing he wanted to do was sit.

Dr. Smith nodded. "I don't blame you." He sat back in his chair. A trace of a smile emerged from behind the beard. "You know, I almost thought Plan F had failed. I was beginning to think I'd never meet you. And now, here you are — grown, handsome, strong — exactly the way your father imagined you would be. And of all times for you to come!"

Ryu couldn't stand it any longer. "Please, Doctor Smith," he pleaded. "Tell me what I'm doing here. Tell me what happened to my father!"

"Very well, my boy." Dr. Smith picked up a pipe from his desk and stood up. He began pacing the room, every once in a while taking a deep puff. "To begin with, I'm not Doctor Smith at all — at least I wasn't until Plan F took effect thirteen years ago." He stopped and looked Ryu in the eye. "Ryu, my real name is Randolph Wimple."

He went on without stopping for an hour. He told all about the expedition thirteen years ago, about the tablet, the inscription, the fearsome creature whose shield was marked with a *J*, the thugs at the hotel.

Before his ears, Ryu's father was coming to life. He could imagine his dad sacrificing himself for Dr. Wimple and the statues. He could picture the fight with the lightning-grabbing monster in the jungle.

Yet somehow he still couldn't believe that his father had lost. Even though he'd never met his dad, he felt that he *knew* him. And the man that he knew wouldn't have let himself be killed.

Ryu put the thought out of his mind. It was a pipe dream. All that mattered was vengeance.

"And so," Dr. Smith said, "we had thought of six emergency plans in advance. Plan F was only to be used in case of extreme danger. That is to say, if the mission was a failure and one of us didn't survive — and if there was a chance of retaliation. In Plan F, the survivor would change his identity and relocate. We chose our names in advance — mine would be Walter Smith."

"And that's why I was able to locate you," Ryu said. "The note he left me was to be opened only if Plan F was in effect."

"A smart man, your dad," Dr. Smith replied. "In the midst of battle against that *thing*, he had enough wits about him to call for the Plan. He was smart enough to realize that someone might try to come after the statues — and he knew that someday you'd find me."

"The Light statue," Ryu suddenly said.

"The one that wasn't stolen. Do you have it?"

Dr. Smith pointed to a painting on the wall. "Behind that painting, there is a very secure wall safe. The Light statue has been there for twelve years, ever since I got my job here. I have reason to believe that there are forces who would like to have the statue, but they haven't been able to track me down. Perhaps they're still looking for a man named Wimple."

"Who would they be? Art collectors?"

Dr. Smith moved closer to Ryu. His voice suddenly became hushed. "Ryu, I have done much research since my expedition with your father. Back then, I laughed at the idea of a sleeping demon. I have since found that it *does* exist!"

Ryu gave him a skeptical look.

"I'm not a crackpot, Ryu. Far from it. The Demon lies in a huge rock mesa near the Peruvian Andes. I've also studied all the inscriptions and legends that pertain to Shinobi's fight in the thirteenth century — and I have calculated that the Demon is scheduled to awake soon. The time of the Dark Moon is near!"

The man must be shell-shocked, Ryu thought. Still, there was something so cool and rational in his voice . . .

"How near?" he asked.

There was a glint in Dr. Smith's eye.

"This is why your visit today is so re-markable. If my figures are correct, the day of the Dark Moon — the seven hundredth anniversary of the Demon's hiberna-tion — will occur *tomorrow*."

Ryu let that sink in. It seemed too unreal, too much like a fairy tale. "So what does that mean, Doctor Smith? The world is going to just explode or something?"

Dr. Smith smiled. "No. Tomorrow you and I can celebrate in your father's name. The world will be safe, as long as I have the Light statue, away from the temple."

Ryu lifted his sack and put it on Dr. Smith's desk. "For what it's worth," he said, lifting out the shining black figurine, "you now have both statues."

Dr. Smith stared. His jaw went slack. Slowly he approached it with disbelieving eyes. "How did you get this?" he said, his voice barely audible.

"Package for Doctor Smith!" a voice shouted at the doorway.

A helmeted postal worker walked in, carrying a shoulder sack. He walked briskly toward the desk.

"Oh!" Dr. Smith exclaimed, jumping with surprise. "I wasn't expecting — "

The man threw down a clipboard. "Sign here."

The statue was now shielded from Ryu by the man's body. Ryu began walking around the desk. He didn't want to let the figurine out of his sight.

As Dr. Smith grabbed a pen from his pocket, the man bolted for the door. "See ya, fellas!" he called out.

The Dark statue was gone.

GAME HINT

To beat Bloody Malth, get right next to him and start throwing your small star (don't stop). When you run out of stars, run up and use your sword.

CHAPTER 9

"Get him, Ryu!" Dr. Smith called out.

Ryu was already out the door. The "postal worker" had run to the left — and he was fast. Ryu raced after him.

As the two of them barreled through the hallways, frightened passersby clung to the walls. Inside archaeology classrooms, students looked up from their stone relics. Inside anthropology classrooms, they looked up from their skeletons.

The thief disappeared around a corner. Ryu could hear a voice yelling, "Hey, what are you doing with my — "

Ryu raced around the same corner at top speed — and wished he hadn't.

He tried to stop, but it was too late. He slammed into a wide, wheeled cart covered by a green tarpaulin. The thief had pushed it in his path.

With a deafening clatter, objects fell to the floor from under the tarp. At the last moment, Ryu managed to roll away.

To his left, a human jawbone shattered. Behind him, a skull bounced without breaking. A thigh bone just missed hitting his arm.

When Ryu jumped to his feet, the floor was littered with pieces of ancient skeletons. The thief's footsteps clattered in the distance.

The man who had been pulling the cart looked stunned. Before he could say a word, Ryu said, "I'm with Doctor Smith!"

He tore off down the hall. Ahead of him was the building's lobby. Through a plate-glass window, Ryu could see the thief sprinting across the lawn.

He pushed through the door. His legs hammered the ground as he ran. But the thief was already through the main gate. The two guards were just looking at him, bewildered.

"Stop him!" Ryu yelled.

There was a squeal of tires. A black Lamborghini pulled away from a hidden spot behind the gate. It left a cloud of dust as it sped away.

Ryu ran right past the guards, who still hadn't decided what to do. He reached into a pocket near his chest. His fingers closed around a razor-sharp *shuriken*. The Ninja Throwing Star was small, but deadly accurate.

He veered to his left around the dust cloud. When the car was in view, he let loose a powerful throw.

The *shuriken* whistled as it sliced the air. It disappeared into the dust cloud — and imbedded itself in the left rear tire of the getaway car.

With a shriek of rubber against blacktop, the car skidded wildly. It turned a complete circle and crashed into a ditch by the side of the road.

Instantly the two front doors opened. The driver bolted to the right, into the desert. The thief emerged from the passenger side, holding the statue.

Ryu pulled out another *shuriken*. "I never miss," he called out.

The thief believed him. Panic bleached his face. He dropped the statue and ran.

Ryu considered chasing him, but didn't. The Dark statue was his again, and that was all that mattered.

He bent over and picked it up.

The security guards ran up behind him. "Who was that guy?" one of them asked.

"Beats me," Ryu replied. He examined the car, memorized the license plate. "He tried to steal a relic from the archaeology department."

"That was some display," the other guard said. "You ever want a job, you ought to get in touch with our boss."

"Thanks," Ryu said with a smile. He walked back across the campus, holding the Dark statue tightly.

Back in the archaeology building, Dr. Smith's door was closed. Ryu knocked.

There was no answer. Ryu hoped that he hadn't gone off to a class or a conference. He tried the doorknob.

It turned easily. Ryu opened the door.

Dr. Smith was there, all right. On the floor. Unconscious.

Papers were strewn around him. His shirt was ripped, his glasses torn off. In his right hand was a glass paperweight, a weapon he probably hadn't had a chance to use.

Ryu rushed to his side. "Doctor Smith!" he called, gently slapping the older man's face. "Are you all right?"

Dr. Smith's eyes slowly opened and then shut. "Sssaaaaaaaffff," he moaned.

"What's that?" Ryu asked, relieved to hear his voice.

The professor gritted his teeth with the pain. "The safe," he muttered, trying to crane his head toward the back wall.

Ryu looked up. Where the painting had been, there was now a hole. A jagged, empty hole, surrounded by a ring of black.

"The Light statue," Ryu said under his breath.

"They . . . they took it!" Dr. Smith grimaced as the words eked out of his mouth.

"Who did?" Ryu asked.

The answer came from the doorway.

"Follow us, please."

Ryu whirled around. Three men stood there, each wearing gray suits.

Each holding a pistol.

CHAPTER 10

"Where are you taking me?" Ryu demanded for what felt like the hundredth time. The handcuffs bit into his wrists as he was helped out of the limousine.

"This way," came the gruff answer. Which was two words more than any of the three men had said during the entire trip from Galesburg.

With a hand gripping each of his shoulders, Ryu walked reluctantly across the parking lot toward a long, low adobe building. They were in the middle of nowhere, a flat landscape of cactus and snakeweed.

They went into the building and entered an elevator. An elevator, in a two-story building. Ryu wondered why they hadn't taken the stairs.

It wasn't long before he realized why. They weren't going up at all. The elevator began plunging downward.

And downward ... and downward ...

After a minute or so, it stopped. The door opened, and a blast of cool air rushed in.

They walked through a brightly lit corridor to an unmarked door. One of the gray-suited men knocked. "We have the kid, sir," he said loudly.

"Ah, good! Come in!" came a voice from within.

The office was huge. As Ryu was led in, he couldn't help but look around at the high-tech gadgetry that festooned the walls. Rear-projection video screens, monitors, holographic maps.

The only thing that wasn't made of plastic, glass, or steel was a polished wooden desk in the middle of the room.

Behind it was a man of about thirty with blond hair and a bland smile. "Foster's the name," he said. His eyes rested on Ryu's for a moment, as if he were reading a message in them. Then he turned to the other men. "The handcuffs aren't necessary. I would like to shake this young man's hand."

One of the guards unlocked the cuffs. Foster leaned over his desk, extending his arm. Ryu didn't take it.

Without a trace of surprise, Foster said, "You handled the Jaquio's men with great skill, Ryu."

Ryu narrowed his eyes. "Where am I?" he asked. "How do you know my name? And who is the Jaquio?"

Foster looked over Ryu's shoulder and

made a small hand gesture. Immediately the guards left the room.

"In answer to your first question," he said, "You are in a CIA outpost that very few people have ever seen. In answer to your second question, I know your name because many years ago your father was involved in trying to discover something of great importance to national security. We tried to tail him, but he eluded our agents in the Amazon jungle. He just . . . disappeared, as you know. Likewise Doctor Wimple — or so we thought."

Ryu felt a shudder. How could this man be talking so coldly, so businesslike, about *his father!*

Foster began pacing. "You see, the moment you made your plane reservation, it appeared in our computer files. For years we suspected that *someone* in your family would come after Doctor Hayabusa. What we didn't suspect was that you would lead us straight to Doctor Wimple, in his new disguise. Your friend, Doctor Wimple/Smith, has been a very crafty fellow. He's conducted his research in the Amazon using different names, sending other archaeologists. He must have suspected that someone was keeping an eye on him."

"So why did you attack him in his own office?" Ryu shot back angrily. "You could have just told him what was going on."

Foster shook his head. "That wasn't us, Ryu. That was the work of a criminal mastermind named Guardia de Mieux, otherwise known as the Jaquio.. We have reason to believe the Jaquio has control of the Temple of Darkness."

"The *what?*" Ryu replied.

"It's where the Demon lives — inside a great rock formation. For years we have been trying to get inside, but the Jaquio has thwarted us. He's amassing all the evil power he can. He is performing rituals, training armies of impossible strength — all in a fanatic quest to take over the world. We believe he is determined to harness the energy of the Demon when it awakes."

"But he can't," Ryu said. "The Demon will sleep as long as the statues are away."

"Exactly. And we have been trying to collect both of them for safekeeping. Years ago, we managed to get hold of the Dark statue. We planted it on you in the hope that you would lead us to the Light one." He sighed. "We didn't suspect the Jaquio would be on our tail."

"Wait a second," Ryu said. "The statue was *planted* on me?"

A voice behind him answered, "That's right, Ryu."

Ryu spun around. Standing in the doorway was the young woman who had shot him.

"You," he said under his breath. "You're working for *them*."

"Them is *us*," Foster cut in. "We're the good guys, Ryu."

"But she shot me!" Ryu protested.

"For your own protection," the young woman said. As she walked toward the desk, she explained, "Those men from the bar were dangerous. You were hopelessly outnumbered. My gun was loaded with tranquilizer darts; they dissolved in your skin without leaving a trace. But the shots scared off your attackers."

"I could have handled them," Ryu said. "I'm a Ninja black belt. Couldn't you see my outfit?"

The young woman shrugged. "I thought it was a high-fashion statement."

"So you brought me to CIA headquarters and gave me the Dark statue — "

"A replica," Foster corrected him. "We didn't want to risk anyone stealing the real one, but we thought you might need something to prove your identity to Doctor Smith."

"In other words," Ryu said, "you abducted me, used me as your means of tracking down Doctor Smith, and caused me to chase the Jaquio's goons over a worthless statue — which forced me to be away from Doctor Smith while he was attacked. All that, so you could get the Light statue, which was taken from under your noses anyway! Good work, guys!"

Foster shook his head and grimaced. "I'm afraid you're right. Even the most sophisticated organizations bungle things up from time to time. That's why we need your help."

"Why should I help you?"

"You're an exceptional fighter, Ryu. I could tell by the way you went after the Jaquio's men. And if you truly are a Ninja, you'll be able to penetrate the Jaquio's lair."

"Perhaps a Ninja would have the understanding of the Jaquio's mystical powers," the young woman added. "Ordinary forces have been helpless."

"Remember, Ryu," Foster said, "he has the Light statue now, and we must retrieve it before tomorrow! Of course, we will pay you for your work."

Ryu looked from Foster to the young woman. He had come to America to carry out his father's wishes, not to get involved in covert government operations. And not to be bought!

"What if I say no?" Ryu said defiantly.

Foster's face instantly grew cold. When he looked at Ryu, his eyes were like lasers. "My young friend," he said, "you don't want to know the answer to that."

CHAPTER 11

"It's down there!"

"What?" Ryu leaned toward the pilot of the tiny CIA plane. The propeller noise was making it almost impossible to hear anything.

"I said it's down there!"

Ryu looked out the window. Below him, the dense South American jungle swept by like a greenish-black carpet. Just beyond its border, there was a long, barren plain.

"Where?" Ryu shouted.

"On the plain! See the really tall rock plateau?"

Ryu nodded. He could see an enormous, craggy rock growth that jutted up like a mountain with its top shaved off.

"You'd better go now!" the pilot yelled. "I have just enough fuel to get me back!"

Ryu checked the straps on his parachute. The wind would carry him into the jungle, not the plain. From above, the treetops looked like a perfect cushion, but he knew how dangerous it really was. After traveling by jeep, ultrasonic jet, and prop plane, Ryu felt weary. Even a Ninja could break his legs falling from a tree.

Looking over his shoulder, Ryu gave a quick salute to the pilot. He tapped his sword for good luck, then jumped.

Almost instantly, the propeller noise faded. The wind boxed his ears. When he looked down, he saw the dense jungle vegetation rushing toward him.

At just the right time, he pulled the rip cord. He grunted as the unfolding parachute jerked him upward.

Then, slowly, he sank into the jungle.

He landed gently in a small clearing. The ground was soft and springy from centuries of fallen leaves. Unbuckling his straps, he ditched the parachute and walked in the direction of the plain.

The overgrown jungle blocked out the bright sunshine he'd seen only minutes ago. Using his Dragon Sword, he slashed his way through the twisting vines.

Around him, the screams of birds and monkeys were like tortured cries for help. Sometimes they sounded miles away. Sometimes they sounded as if they were right over his shoulder. More than once, he would spin around to slay an approaching beast, only to find it was nowhere near him.

It was the silent animals that really

worried him. The smart ones, the ones who just lay waiting for their prey. Did the Amazon have animals like that?

A rustle in a nearby bush answered his question.

With a roar that turned Ryu's blood to ice, a cougar leaped out of hiding.

Ryu froze. It was against his personal code to kill a living thing unless his life was in mortal danger.

It was. And Ryu was too late.

As the cougar attacked, it bared its razor-sharp teeth — teeth that made the Dragon Sword look like a putty knife.

GAME HINT

To beat Jaquio, use the Art of the Fire Wheel and shoot him once, run to the left and shoot him again. Then run to the right and repeat, again and again.

CHAPTER 12

Chi power.

The words flashed into Ryu's brain. It was the secret mental discipline known only to the Ninjas, the ability to cloud a person's mind. Using *chi* power, a Ninja could appear invisible to an opponent.

But would it work with an animal?

Ryu used a *yoko-aruki* sidestep. The cougar narrowly missed him, landing gracefully on all fours. With a deep growl, it turned toward Ryu again. Its eyes were bloodshot, its mouth drooling.

Ryu looked into its eyes. He concentrated hard, blanking his mind of all but the *chi* energy.

It came to him from the ages. It came to him as a full-grown source of power, born generations ago in the minds of the original Ninja warriors. With their rugged training, attacking under cover of darkness with the power of *chi*, the Ninja avenged the reign of terror of the all-powerful samurai.

Some laughed at the idea of *chi*; it was all psychological, they said.

Whatever it was, it was working.

The cougar's growl softened to a whimper. Before Ryu's eyes, it began sniffing the ground. It sensed Ryu was there, but it couldn't see him.

Ryu walked away without making a sound. Before long, he came to the end of the jungle. The plain stretched out before him. All around, the earth was flat and arid. Clumps of scrub brush dotted the landscape, and lizards skittered about.

In the distance, like a pyramid that had been heaved from the earth itself, stood the Temple of Darkness.

It was more awesome than the photos Foster had shown him. Its ledges of brown rock were jagged and brutal. It cast the only shadow for miles around. No plants, not even the tiniest patch of grass, grew anywhere near it. The wind that whistled around it seemed to be saying *sssstay away, sssstay away*!

As Ryu walked toward it, he could feel its energy. It was as if the rock itself were breathing. It seemed to push at Ryu; several times he found himself veering away. He could tell that any ordinary person would have changed course by now.

But he was far from ordinary. And something inside of him was telling him to go onward. He was there for a reason, and it wasn't because the CIA had sent him.

No, the CIA was merely a step along the way toward Ryu's ultimate destiny. At the end of his path, Ryu would find out what had happened to his father. Of this, if nothing else, he was certain.

When Ryu reached the base of the mesa, the force was almost unbearable. It felt as if he were a tiny north magnet trying to touch the north end of the world's largest magnetic field. He fought against it. He looked for a way in.

Several yards away was a tall, triangular gash in the rock. He walked toward it, then entered.

The darkness was total. Pitch-black. His footsteps echoed as he walked blindly forward. A pinpoint of light shone from around a corner. It led him to a hallway, then a room.

Lit by thin shafts of sunlight through cracks in the ceiling, the room was narrow and long. It was a natural cavern, and its cool, dry air chilled Ryu to the bone. A set of train tracks ran straight down the center. Where the tracks ended, an old, rusted coal car sat. Its black paint job was fuzzy gray from years of dust. Ryu reached inside and wiped a layer of grime off the wooden seat. Then he hopped in, wondering if there were any controls.

There didn't have to be. Immediately the car lurched forward. Ryu was thrown back. He clutched the sides of the car.

With sudden acceleration, it sped away, leaving the room behind. It climbed and climbed, into a grotto, then another cavern.

Ryu looked down. The tracks were elevated high above the ground now, on a spindly wood scaffolding that creaked with the strain. Below him was a pool of black, stagnant liquid.

The liquid began to move — or rather, what was in the liquid moved. Ryu's eyes widened. It had a long, curved body. With sharp fins. And sharper teeth. And mocking eyes that seemed to beckon him downward.

The car was shuddering. Ryu looked ahead. Suddenly the forward momentum stopped.

A scream ripped from his lungs to his mouth. The tracks had ended. He was plunging down, into the gaping jaws below!

CHAPTER 13

Inches from Ryu's face, the broken ends of the scaffold raced by. He jumped from the falling train car, reaching desperately with his hands.

His fingers closed around a thin slat of wood. The momentum of his body carried him around the slat. He swung as if on a parallel bar. The scaffolding swayed and squeaked. Splinters of rotted wood fell into the black lagoon with hollow *plup*, *plup* sounds.

When he stopped, he looked down again. A few feet below him, the train car was floating on its side.

Slowly, a long, black tentacle rose out of the murk. It was coated with oily sludge, and flaps of skin hung loose. It wrapped itself twice around the train car. Then it contracted. With a sudden, violent splitting sound, the car smashed in half.

Ryu let go with his left hand, then grabbed the wooden slat directly above.

Crrrrack. It split off and tumbled downward.

This wasn't going to be easy.

With painstaking care, Ryu began climbing. He went from slat to slat, testing each one. It seemed to take hours, but he eventually clambered to the top.

Ahead of him, the tracks continued through a large hole in the cavern wall. Ryu began walking. With each step, the scaffold shook. He extended his arms to the side, like a tightrope walker. Below him, the monster snarled and jumped, unhappy with his dinner of wood and steel. It whipped its tail against the scaffold.

Spprrrroing!

The scaffold bowed to one side. Ryu almost lost his balance. He had to make time now. Quickly he scampered toward the hole.

Spprrrroing!

He had only a few feet to go. The wooden slats weren't going to hold the stress much longer . . .

KRRRRRROCKKKK!

The room echoed with the sound of splitting wood. Like a house of toothpicks, the scaffold collapsed.

CHAPTER 14

Ryu's fingers clung to the edge of the wall opening. His feet dangled above the heap of fallen wood. He hoisted himself up and peered inside. The first thing he checked was the floor. It was solid. He'd be able to walk.

The second thing he noticed was an eerie flaming lantern on the wall. He walked toward it. Without knowing why, he felt his hand traveling to his belt.

The Dragon Sword was summoning him.

During his years of Ninja training, he had learned not to question the urges that came over him at times like this. There were always reasons.

He pulled the sword. At the same time, he heard a noise above him. A loud *caw*, like a crow.

He looked up at the noise. It wasn't a crow. Far from it.

As a child, Ryu learned that many scientists believed certain dinosaurs had evolved into birds. He had always doubted that. Not anymore.

What flew toward him had no feathers. Its skin was brown and leathery. Its wings stretched out on either side like two fleshy curtains. And its teeth were long white spikes that jutted from the edge of its beak.

With another shrieking cackle, it swooped toward Ryu. But he didn't defend himself. Instead, he stepped toward the lantern. He fought against the voice inside him that cried out, "Fight back!" That was a human, mortal voice. What was driving him to the lantern was deeper than that. A spiritual force.

"Why?" the mortal voice begged. Ryu ignored it.

He raised his arm high. The tip of the Dragon Sword glinted in the reflected light of the lantern. The flying creature raced toward him like a bullet.

Ryu slashed the lantern with his sword.

The lantern? What about the bird?

He gritted his teeth, expecting the lantern to shatter. Instead, it dissolved. Just disappeared.

The Dragon Sword glowed amber. Ryu felt a surge of energy.

YEEEEEEAAAAACKKK! The bird

was upon him. He thrust with the Dragon Sword. Once.

All that touched him was a shower of sparks. The bird fell to the ground, a tangled mass of wires and computer chips.

It wasn't an ancient species at all. The Jaquio must be a high-tech wizard, along with his other powers.

Ryu walked to the end of the chamber, where a ladder led to a trapdoor in the roof. He climbed up and pushed the door open.

A cold wind from the Peruvian Andes blasted his face as he lifted himself through. He was on a narrow ledge of the rock mesa, looking away from the jungle.

Shhhhisssshhh! A lock of Ryu's hair suddenly fell to the ground, neatly cut off.

He whirled around. Standing before him was a hooded Ninja warrior, holding a gleaming steel *Ninja-to* sword. Around his waist was a black belt.

"My name is Barbarian," the man said. "I have been looking forward to a challenge like this."

Ryu unsheathed his sword. The two of them faced each other. Each expected the other to begin. Ryu knew that a battle like this did not depend on physical power. Whoever had the spiritual edge would win.

He balanced his weight carefully. An image of the lantern flashed through his mind. The lantern had given him strength. He had looked to it the way a man would look out of the darkness into the light. In his soul, he believed it would give him power, and it did. *This* was strength of the spirit. If he still had it, he could make the first move.

He slashed. The Dragon Sword whistled as it cut the air. Black belt or not, Barbarian had no time to react. And before Ryu's thrust had completed its arc, the warrior was gone. Like the monstrous bird, he had just vanished.

Ryu walked along the ledge. He followed it around the mesa until he saw another trapdoor. This one was larger, and bright light shone from within.

As he stepped closer, a deep, rumbling laugh welled up.

"Welcome, young soldier! Please do drop in."

The voice was like the scraping of cement against metal. It made Ryu grit his teeth. Cautiously he approached the hole and looked in.

The harsh glare made him turn his eyes. He squinted and tried to take in the astonishing sight below him. It was a more like an oversized jewel box than a room. The walls were made of carved gold, studded with diamonds that threw webs of light around the room. The floor was polished platinum, decorated with occasional ruby and emerald tiles.

"No gawking, please. Would you like to enter my humble abode?"

Ryu still couldn't see where the voice was coming from. He dropped through the hole, landing on one of the ruby tiles. At the far end of the room, there was a platform at the top of three steps carpeted with mink. On the platform was a throne that dazzled with thousands of inlaid jewels. Sitting on the platform, his chalk-white face framed by a hood of spun gold, was the Jaquio.

"So this is the first intrepid soul to have penetrated into my chamber!" the Jaquio roared. "Ha! You are but a child, with a child's luck!"

Ryu drew his sword. "I'm not afraid of you, Jaquio!"

"Then you will go to your death peacefully!"

Behind Ryu, there was a sudden thump. He turned to see a door opening in the gilded wall. "Let go of me, turkey!" came a familiar voice.

A heavily muscled guard came through the door. Flailing in his arms, trying to pry away from his stranglehold, was the red-haired girl from the CIA!

"How did she get in here?" the Jaquio demanded.

"She followed behind the boy, Your Omniscience," the guard said. "He laid several rooms to waste. I caught her as she was trying to climb the Great Ladder!"

"Where is your weapon, dunderhead?" the Jaquio bellowed.

The guard drew a gun from his belt. The girl went stiff with fright.

The Jaquio laughed again. **"Now, my young swordsman, give me the Dark statue, or your devoted lady fair will come to an unseemly end!"**

Fine, Ryu thought. The Jaquio didn't know that Foster had given him only a replica of the statue. The problem was, would he be fooled long enough for the time of the Dark Moon to pass?

Trying to look defeated and hopeless, Ryu lay the statue at the Jaquio's feet.

"On your knees!" the Jaquio thundered.

Ryu ground his teeth. It repulsed him to kowtow to this barbarian, but if it would save a life . . .

As his knees touched the ground, the girl blurted out: "Ryu, no! The statue is real! I gave you the real one by mistake — *that's* why they sent me after you!"

Those were the last words Ryu heard as a trick door fell open beneath him.

CHAPTER 15

Ryu hurtled downward into the darkness. He landed hard on a rock floor, tumbling end over end. When he came to rest, he was in another chamber, wide and empty. Blazing torches threw patches of light around, casting bizarre shadows.

For the first time in a while, Ryu had a chance to think. He had to get back to the Jaquio. With both statues, the evil creature would surely be able to take over the world.

Ryu's head was jangling with questions. Who was the red-haired girl? Was she really a CIA agent, or was she in cahoots with the Jaquio? Maybe she was a double agent. But for whom?

Was she telling the truth? Was *anybody* telling the truth?

Ryu didn't have time to find any answers. A spark shot out of the wall next to him. He dove away.

A familiar object clattered to the ground. A *shuriken*.

Across the room, where no one had been

standing a moment ago, there was a hulking figure. His face was covered by a death mask, and sharp spikes protruded from his uniform at the shoulders and wrists.

"Hey, don't worry, man," he said in a raspy voice, thick with a New York accent. "I wouldn't do nothing to you while you wasn't looking. I wait till people look me in the eye before I kill them."

"Nice of you," Ryu said dryly.

"Hey, don't mention it," the man said. "When Bomberhead wants to kill, he kills clean."

With that, Bomberhead began swinging his right arm around. His fingers were gripping the end of a powerful chain. On the other end was a long, two-headed sickle.

Ryu's mind raced. Using *chi* power would be too risky. Bomberhead must have been a master of *chi* power himself; he had prevented Ryu from seeing him at first.

The sickle swung wildly in a circle. Any second now, Bomberhead would let loose.

Anger welled up inside of Ryu. He was failing. He had let down Dr. Smith, the CIA was using him, his life was in danger, and he hadn't come close to finding out anything about his father.

Ryu was desperate. It was time for the Art of the Fire Wheel.

Never had Ryu attempted this dangerous special form. He had learned it at the end of a training session — a session in which he had gotten so furious that steam had begun to rise around him.

Use your anger, his instructor had said. *Turn it into a weapon.* He had shown Ryu how, and the results were so powerful Ryu vowed never to try it unless he had no other choice.

Now he had no other choice.

He let his rage rise to a fever pitch. He felt his skin begin to turn hot. Then came the smoke . . .

Bomberhead's eyes were growing wide with confusion. He swung the chain and sickle faster, preparing for a mighty throw.

Was it going to work . . . or would it only be smoke? Ryu thought about his dad, about the senseless death he must have suffered.

Fwwosshhh! There is was. The fire. It surrounded Ryu's body, turned him into a human ball of flames.

Bomberhead's swing faltered. He stood staring, slack-jawed.

With a dull *thunk*, the sickle fell to the ground. Ryu stepped forward. The flames leapt from his body. They encased Bomberhead. There was a burst of light like a supernova.

In the next instant, Bomberhead was gone.

The flames flickered, then died. Ryu collapsed to the ground in pain. He wasn't used to the Art of the Fire Wheel. He hoped he would never have to get used to it. It had worked, but he felt completely sapped of energy.

Out of the corner of his eye, he saw a door at the other end of the room. Maybe it led back to the Jaquio.

He struggled to his feet and dragged himself across the cavern. Bats squeaked above him, as if laughing. He knew his strength would return; it would just take a little time. And during that time he might as well be moving. As long as he didn't run into someone like Bomberhead . . .

He grabbed the knob and yanked the door open.

"Agghh!" An involuntary cry escaped from Ryu's throat. There was someone in the doorway.

Someone huge. Someone with a sharp butterfly knife in each hand, and a bloodthirsty grin on his face.

"I understand you defeated my friends Barbarian and Bomberhead," the fearsome creature said, raising his knives. "Welcome, my friend, to the major leagues."

CHAPTER 16

"Who are you?" Ryu asked. He was weak. He had to stall for time.

"I am called Basaquer, the third of the Jaquio's bosses."

"How many of you *are* there?" Ryu groaned.

Basaquer laughed. "Four, but that does not matter. You will not get past me, I assure you. No one ever has."

With that, Basaquer casually tossed one of the knives. With incredible precision, it flew toward Ryu's Dragon Sword. The knife blade missed his hand by millimeters. Its shank caught on the sword handle, tearing the sword away from Ryu. He watched helplessly as his weapon clanked to the floor near an ancient, abandoned hourglass.

"Get it," Basaquer said. "Get the sword and bring it to me. And don't try anything funny, because you know what I can do!"

Ryu turned to the sword. His defenses were down. He felt too weak to use *chi* power and didn't dare use the Art of the Fire Wheel again.

He bent to pick up the sword. He could see its tip mirrored in the smooth surface of the hourglass.

Suddenly he knew what to do. It was a crazy thought, almost a hallucination. Ryu almost ignored it. But his instructor Akira had always told him: *The spirit of a Ninja runs deep, ready to refresh the thirsting soul.* Now as before, Ryu knew to trust his instinct.

The hourglass. He had to touch the hourglass with the Dragon Sword.

His fingers gripped the sword handle. He lifted it. As he stood up, he brought the tip close to the glass surface.

"Hurry up!" Basaquer commanded. "I have no time for — "

Zzzhhhhapp!

There was a flash of blue light. Basaquer stood in the doorway, frozen in midsentence. Ryu wondered what he was staring at.

Then he noticed that all sounds had stopped. No whoosh of wind currents, no squeaking of bats. He looked up.

There *were* bats, three of them. They were suspended in midair, as if by strings. What had happened? Ryu glanced at the hourglass again, and it suddenly came to him. Time was standing still. It was allowing

Ryu to attack despite his weakened state.

He did. His thrust wasn't as strong as usual, but it didn't need to be. Basaquer, the look of impatience still locked onto his face, disintegrated without a fight.

Around him, the bats began to squeak again. A droplet of limewater that had been hanging in midfall now splashed onto a stalagmite.

Ryu went through the door. It led to some sort of a tunnel. Actually, a *pipe* was a better description. Judging from the smell, it was once part of a sewer that had fallen into disuse. It was plenty wide for a human to walk upright, but it was lit only by the weak light through the open door behind him.

Ryu walked along, hoping it would lead to the outside. Then he could mount a new attack on the Temple, a smarter attack.

He felt his strength slowly returning. Ahead of him, there was a weak shaft of light coming from the top of the pipe. As he got closer, he saw that the light outlined the shape of a square. Below it was a small ladder.

Bingo. It was exactly what Ryu wanted. He climbed up the ladder and pushed against the door.

Creeeeeak.

There were no hinges. Instead, the entire square lifted upward. It was made of heavy stone, and Ryu had to push hard. Light began to stream in, along with the lush, humid smells of the jungle.

Shcrrraaawwwwwwwwk — clunk!

He pushed the stone aside and stuck his head out. He was at the edge of a small clearing. The grass was brown and the dirt hard. Everything had been made dull by the intense sunlight — except for the square stone. Ryu couldn't help notice the gold inlays that sharply reflected the light. There were intricate figurines arranged in some sort of ancient message.

Something else caught his eye. Across the clearing there was a larger stone tablet, carved with tightly spaced words.

He wasn't sure why, but somehow this place seemed familiar. Surely he'd never been here before . . .

He walked closer to the tablet, but a horrible, loud voice made him stop short.

"Welcome, my friends, to the home of Bloody Malth. I'm glad you're here. I've been starved for victims!"

The words shook the ground. Suddenly Ryu's sword flew out of its scabbard and into the woods. He turned around, stunned.

What he saw was half human, half machine. A cyborg. Its chest muscles seemed sculpted out of metal. There were three claws on its feet, and a horned mask on its face. It held a sword in its right hand. In its left, it wielded a heavy metal shield as if it were plastic.

A shield that displayed the letter *J*.

"J for Jaquio," Ryu said fearlessly. "Is that so you don't lose it?"

"A despicable sense of humor. I guess it runs in the family."

Ryu's stomach flipflopped. He felt the blood rush from his head. He knew why the place seemed familiar.

The stone . . . like a tombstone. The clearing. The inscribed tablet. The shield marked with a *J*.

How could he have been so slow to figure it out? No, he hadn't been here before — but his father had. To the last detail, it was the exact place that Dr. Smith had described at the university. The place where Dr. Ken Hayabusa had died.

"I know who you are." The words were wrenched out of the deepest part of Ryu's soul. His eyes glared with the pent-up anger of a lifetime. *"You killed my father!"*

"HAAAH-HA-HA-HA!" Malth's laughter resounded like rifle shots. **"Where is your sense of humor now, young Hayabusa? I find this situation extremely funny! In fact, you might say the air crackles with comedy!"**

Thunder sounded in the distance. The warrior slowly raised its arm.

"You haven't seen anything yet. Here is something that will electrify you!"

Malth cackled at its own joke as a bolt of lightning split the sky, stretching toward the creature's upheld sword.

GAME HINT

To beat the Bomberhead, get next to him, duck, and hit him with your sword.

CHAPTER 17

"Electrify! HAAWW-HAW-HAW-HAW-HAW!"

Malth guffawed like someone who had discovered laughing for the first time. The sound was ugly, awkward. Its abdomen shook. Behind its mask, its eyes were closed.

This was Ryu's only chance. He leaped forward.

DZZZZZZIT!

The lightning sparked as it made contact with the tip of Malth's sword. Ryu grabbed its arm. He felt the current surge through him.

Malth stopped laughing. The electricity sputtered, then died. Ryu twisted Malth's wrist downward. "What the — " it began to say.

But that was all Malth could get out. With all his strength, Ryu turned the sword and plunged it deep into an unshielded spot near Malth's collarbone.

Acrid, black smoke billowed from the hole made by the sword. Sparks shot out from Malth's complex inner machinery. From its mouth came a mechanical squawk. It sank to the ground.

"Impossible," Malth said. "This was not programmed!"

Ryu leaned over the dying cyborg. It was hard to believe that this malfunctioning hunk of hardware once dealt a death blow to his father. If only he could go into the past and tell his dad about Malth's fatal weakness . . .

"I guess your human side got the better of you," Ryu said softly.

He looked away and sighed. Was this what his whole trip had been about? If he had come to America to avenge his father's death, why did the victory feel so empty?

Through the slits in the mask, Malth's eyes glowered at Ryu. "You think you've avenged your father's death, don't you? You think that when I'm gone, all will be square. Well, you're wrong. For one thing, I can be constructed again. And as for your father, he is still alive — and captive!"

"You lie!" Ryu said. "You're saying that to get the last word in, to give me false hope — to make me return to the Jaquio! Well, I won't give you the satisfaction, Malth! I don't believe you!"

"Very well, then. I shall leave you without mentioning another word. I suppose you don't care enough to know where he is being kept. Why should you care? You never met the man. And besides, he abandoned you."

Ryu's temper broke. He stormed up to Malth and pulled him up by the mask. "You can't talk about my father like that! Tell me where this supposed hiding place is. I will go to it, then defeat the Jaquio. If you've tricked me, it won't matter — you won't be around to gloat!"

Malth tried to laugh, but in his weakened state it was a brittle snicker. "Go back through the opening and follow the tunnel when it forks left. At the end, take the pathway made of black stone. In time, you will come upon a room. If you manage to enter, you will see your father — but it will be the last thing you see!"

With a cough and an electric sputter, Malth fell silent.

CHAPTER 18

Ryu let go of Malth. He felt ripped apart inside. Surely this was a trick. If he followed the path, he would be ambushed. He would be distracted from finding the Jaquio. If he gave in to his emotions, he would be sacrificing the world to a madman the likes of which it had never seen. His father was dead. Impossible as it seemed, he had to face it.

He retrieved his sword. Then he took a deep breath. Above him, the sky was beginning to darken. Just above the horizon, the evening's first star peeked at him, sending a shaft of light so strong that Ryu had to blink. It must have been a trick of the jungle air. He had never seen a color so rich and bright.

Suddenly the words of a poem spilled into his thoughts:

"And when you're lost, my son,
When joy becomes despair,
I'll send a star of deepest gold,
To let you know I'm there."

It was his father's poem, the one he had written in the letter. Ryu felt a knot in his stomach. His eyes began to well.

"Stop," he told himself. This was not a time to succumb to emotion. It was just a coincidence.

Still, what would be the harm of following Malth's instructions? Ryu knew he could survive whatever was thrown his way.

He jumped into the tunnel. The path was exactly as Malth had told him — except for one thing.

There was a guard at the end of the black stone pathway. A guard that walked on four legs and had fangs and growled with an unearthly sound.

Ryu kept his distance at first. He couldn't tell if the creature saw him — its eyes were completely white. As it paced back and forth, Ryu studied its horribly deformed shape. Although its head was a cross between a wolf and a panther, its body was hunched in a permanent crouch, like a frog. Its thigh muscles were the width of tree trunks, and it barely moved its legs when it walked.

Ryu edged closer. He unsheathed his Dragon Sword.

The creature turned to face him. The whites of its eyes shone like beacons. "Who dares challenge Kelbeross?"

Ryu hadn't expected it to talk. He hesitated before speaking, having never addressed an animal before. "I mean to step by, Kelbeross."

"You and what army?" Kelbeross replied. Its upper lip curled backward into a snarl, revealing the full length of its top teeth. A greenish venom dripped from the corners of its mouth. The liquid hissed when it hit the floor, leaving white marks on the stone. Acid, Ryu realized.

"Kelbeross, I don't wish you harm. I mean to enter the room beyond you."

Kelbeross opened his mouth as if to answer. Instead, a stream of acid flew toward Ryu.

Ryu ducked. There was a brief *tssss* as a drop of the liquid touched a few strands of his hair, burning them away.

He crouched low to the ground. Kelbeross eyed him warily. It would be risky to use the Dragon Sword; if Ryu got close enough to strike, Kelbeross would fry him with acid. *Chi* power was out because there were no eyeballs for Ryu to look into.

Ryu was angry. Angry that this poison-drooling monster might be the only thing standing between him and his father — *if* his father was alive.

He was angry that his father might *not* be alive; that this might all be a trick.

His rage was enough to activate the

Art of the Fire Wheel, but he knew he wasn't close enough.

But there was another aspect to the Art of the Fire Wheel, one he had almost forgotten. It was a dangerous, harmful technique that could backfire. Akira had warned Ryu against using it until he was a little bit older.

Tsssshhhhhhhhh! A wisp of smoke drifted past his nostrils. Another stream of acid had missed him by a millimeter.

Suddenly Ryu felt as if he had aged ten years. If you can hear what I'm thinking, Akira, he thought, give me your blessing.

Ryu let his fury grow. He rolled away as more acid shot toward him. He stood up, thinking about his father, thinking about the condition he might be in if he was still alive. Thinking about the nightmare he had gone through to get this far.

The smoke formed around him. It turned to flame. Kelbeross cocked its head, looking for a moment like an innocent, curious dog. Then it began rolling back its upper lip again.

Ryu rotated his right arm. Small spots of fire followed the path of his hand. They gathered into balls, three of them. The balls grew bigger, brighter, more solid.

With a powerful heave, Ryu flung the fireballs.

The whites of Kelbeross's eyes seemed

to grow whiter. Its tight, snarling lips fell limp.

As the creature disappeared in a burst of light, Ryu thought he heard a final, defenseless whimper.

The hall was clear now. The flames around Ryu flickered out.

But this time, he didn't feel weak. This time, he had a clear pathway to the door toward which Malth had directed him.

It was made of solid steel plates, riveted tightly into a massive structure that stretched upward at least twenty feet. It had been made so that nothing could break in. Or could it have been made so that nothing could break *out?*

Ryu knew one of two things was in store. A reunion with his father — or certain death.

Without a shred of fear, he walked toward the door. With a thrust of the Dragon Sword, he broke the lock.

Taking a deep breath, he opened it.

CHAPTER 19

It was black inside. But that wasn't what made fear pour through Ryu's body.

Deep, snarling breaths echoed off the walls. First they seemed to come from the left, then the right.

Then there was the smell. Ryu had never experienced anything like it. It reminded him of decay, of rotting meat.

He became aware of smoke circling around him, embracing him like ghostly fingers. It was warm, moist, and musty, and it seemed to coat his skin with a film of slime.

But it was the breaths that frightened Ryu the most. They seemed to whisper death; they rattled and wheezed like the last gasps of a doomed person.

If Ryu's father was in here, maybe Ryu didn't want to see him.

"Who — who is here?" Ryu called out. He tried to keep his voice firm, but it came out thin and shaky.

Whatever was in the room belched

another cloud of smoke. Ryu staggered backward, coughing.

"What? Is this the brave boy who stood before the great Jaquio so defiantly only moments ago?" came the Jaquio's voice. It sounded electronically amplified; Ryu guessed it was coming out of speakers. "You seem a different person. Could this be fear I detect?"

"Where is my father, Jaquio?" Ryu shouted.

"Not so fast, my impetuous prisoner!" The Jaquio laughed. "I have much to tell you before you die. Much that concerns you. Perhaps you are not aware of what I have been doing all these years shut up in this temple — only developing the world's most spectacular advances in mind and body control!"

"I couldn't care less, Jaquio!" Ryu retorted. "Just tell me about my father."

"Your father," the Jaquio snapped, "was one of my greatest successes. Malth was right. Doctor Hayabusa is not dead. He has been transformed — we fondly call him the Masked Devil. He is now a killing machine like no other!"

Horror washed over Ryu like a bath of liquid ice. "What are you talking about, you demented creep?"

The hot breath in the room suddenly became a gust of fire and grit. Ryu backed away, covering his eyes.

"Ryu Hayabusa, you're about to meet your match — and guess what!" The Jaquio's deep laughter rumbled through the room. **"He's your own flesh and blood!"**

Ryu stood erect in the darkness. He looked toward the source of the heavy breathing. He strained his eyes, trying to see something, *anything*, in the suffocating darkness.

A word fought its way up from the bottom of his being. It was a name. A name he had never addressed anyone with, never dreamed that he would. Now he would say it for the first time in his life, and it felt wonderful and terrifying at the same time.

"Dad?"

With sudden, blinding harshness, the room was bathed in bright light. Extending from the floor to the ceiling was a horrible mask. It was molded to look like putrid flesh, bubbling over itself, dripping onto the floor. Its eyes were hollow sockets, its nose gnarled and broken. Its mouth was retracted into a grotesque grin, rimmed with knifelike teeth.

Fire whiplashed out of the mouth of the Masked Devil.

Ryu backed away, his skin singed with the flame. And as the mask rushed toward him, flaring its teeth, he heard the Jaquio's voice screaming with sinister glee:

"Happy reunion, father and son!"

CHAPTER 20

Chhhhhossssssssh!

A plume of fire rushed toward Ryu like an exploding star. He dove away. A jolt of pain rushed up from the top of his left *tabi* boot.

It was on fire. He rolled on the ground, smothering the flames. When it was out, the skin of his left calf showed through the scorched hole in his Ninja suit.

The Masked Devil was coming toward him. Its leering face loomed larger, filling the room.

Ryu felt paralyzed. Was this repulsive, slobbering, fire-breathing monster really his father? It *couldn't* be. But what if it was? What if the Jaquio really had the power to make such an incredible transformation? Ryu would have to fight to kill — against his own dad.

There had to be a way to find out the truth. This mask wasn't just a person. There was some kind of power behind it — some force that gave it life. Ryu knew that there was only one hope. One chance to save himself *and* save his father . . . if he existed.

Ryu had to find the source of that power.

He ducked away from another blast. This time, he landed near the door.

The door was still open. He ran through. Behind him, the voice of the Jaquio cackled: **"You can run, Ryu Hayabusa, but you won't get far! You know this is your father! If you come back to get him, you'll die. If you don't come back, I'll get you! And if you were to escape, I'd kill your dad and your redheaded girlfriend!"**

The Jaquio's maniacal laughter pounded in his ears. He ran blindly through the hallway, not knowing where to go. In full stride, he pulled the Dragon Sword from its scabbard. It had saved him when hope had been lost; it had shown him the way. He had faith that now, somehow, it would guide him.

He held out the sword. The tip pointed to the right, down the path of black stone. It seemed to pull on his hand. Ryu smiled. Someone was on his side.

The path wound through the temple, curving, climbing, dipping. Before long Ryu could hear a noise — it was louder than a roar, longer than an explosion, more desperate than a whine. It seemed to penetrate through his skin to his bones.

It came from the end of the corridor, from an open door that sent out a cascade of bright purple light.

Ryu approached the room carefully. The Dragon Sword had not failed him. He couldn't be sure, but this felt like a power source — like a generator that belonged to a great power plant.

When he saw what was inside, he was sure.

The statue was on a pedestal the size of a small house. It towered upward, dominating the room. Its body was like that of a massive, powerful man.

Its face was the face of the Masked Devil.

It opened its mouth. A fireball catapulted out, then another, and another. Ryu jumped aside. By now he was used to that trick.

Or so he thought.

The fireballs should have crashed to the ground, at the spot Ryu had just left. But they didn't.

In front of his disbelieving eyes, they were curving in midair. Defying gravity. They were missiles of death, and they weren't going to stop until they found their victim!

CHAPTER 21

Ryu jumped away, swinging the Dragon Sword wildly.

Ssswaaeesh! Sswaaeesh! Sswaaeesh! The blade sliced through the flaming missiles, disintegrating them.

Ryu wasted no time. He rushed the monster and plunged the Dragon Sword into its side.

A glowing green gelatin spurted out. A droplet landed on Ryu's sleeve. With a puff of smoke and a hiss, a patch of material dissolved.

He withdrew the Dragon Sword and stood back. The goop was now oozing out. The monster's powerful noise was now a sputtering wheeze. Lights flickered and swelled. A fire burst out of the top of the monsters mask.

Then, slowly, it began to melt. The grotesque features of the creature's face became twisted and warped. As it shriveled down into a puddle of molten plastic and mangled machinery, it almost seemed to be smiling.

Ryu flew out of the room. He raced down the corridors, twisting and turning. Ahead of him was the door to the room that had held the Masked Devil.

He suddenly stopped. What would be in there? If the Masked Devil were still alive, it might be waiting in ambush. If it were dead . . . the idea was too horrifying to consider.

Ryu stepped closer. He heard a sound; there was something waiting behind the door. He took out his Dragon Sword again. He leapt into the doorway, poised for battle.

The room was completely dark. He could see nothing.

Then, from below him came a hoarse whisper.

"Ryu?"

There was a dragging noise. On the floor.

Ryu backed away into the corridor. His heart was racing. But he had come so far, through so many disappointments, that he refused to let his emotions take over. "Who are you?" he called out.

"Ryu," the voice repeated.

Out of the blackness, a person pulled himself into the light of the hallway. It was a man, thin and ragged-looking. His hair was shoulder length and sweat soaked, his face unshaven. But when he looked at Ryu, his eyes blazed with a fierce intelligence — and a tenderness that could not have belonged to a total stranger. Ryu had not felt anyone look at him — see him — as deeply as this man did. He seemed to be sizing Ryu up, counting the years.

Ryu tried to say something, but the words choked in his throat. He swallowed and tried again. "Are you my — "

That was all he could get out. The man slowly nodded.

Ryu sank to his knees. He returned the man's deep gaze. He saw the pride that burned within, the grief that spilled from his eyes and spread lines of sadness down his face.

Sadness over the lost years, sadness over having missed his son's life.

"You've come for me, Ryu," Dr. Ken Hayabusa said.

With a grimace, Dr. Hayabusa picked himself up to a kneeling position. A smile struggled across his lips, and the lines of sadness suddenly etched his face with profound joy. Slowly, gently, he opened his arms.

Ryu hesitated. The years of expectation, the violent journey, had steeled him. He felt incapable of emotion.

"Ryu," his father said, "when you were a tiny child, I used to recite a poem to you."

He laughed. "Of course, you wouldn't remember it — "

" 'And when you're lost, my dearest son,' " Ryu said, his voice beginning to crack, " 'When joy becomes despair —' "

Dr. Hayabusa finished for him. " 'I'll send a star of deepest gold, to let you know I'm there.' "

Ryu fell into his father's arms. Somewhere in the dimmest reaches of his memory, he could recall how they had felt. Back then, the arms had supported him, kept his fragile infant body from falling to the ground.

Now, they were adjusting to a new shape, embracing a young man. Ryu had never felt so complete, so strong.

"Oh, please!" the Jaquio's voice blared. **"This display is repulsive!"**

This time, the voice was not coming from a speaker. It was behind them.

The Jaquio was standing in the doorway. His eyes glared with the intensity of a blast furnace, his lips flared back to reveal tightly clamped teeth. He was seething with fury.

Ryu tried to devise a plan. How could he save his father and himself? What would the Jaquio's next move be? Probably a long, gloating speech about the statues. Ryu might be able to use the Art of the Fire Wheel, or —

Without saying another word, the Jaquio thrust his open palm in Ryu's direction. Out of it shot a blazing fireball.

Ryu was caught by surprise. But his father wasn't. Leaping to his feet like the nimble young Ninja he once was, Dr. Hayabusa dove in front of his son.

The fireball caught him full force in the chest. With an anguished cry that sliced through Ryu like a bayonet, he crumbled to the ground.

"Dad!" The scream ripped Ryu's vocal cords. He grabbed his father by the shoulder, tried to lift him up.

But Dr. Hayabusa was limp and motionless. For the first time since Ryu had seen him, he seemed to be at peace.

GAME HINT

On level 6–2, use the 'jump & slash' technique. If you don't want to waste your points, hold down on the cross pad while jumping and using your sword.

CHAPTER 22

Ryu stood up. At his feet was the motionless body of his father. He was gone.

Again.

A lifetime of refusing to believe he was dead. A lifetime of nagging hope, of wondering about the letter. A lifetime of training — just in case.

Well, "just in case" had come. And Ryu's wildest dream had come true. He had met his father.

For about five minutes.

A madman had stolen thirteen years of his father's life, and now that madman had ended it with a flash of temper and a wave of his hand.

Ryu went numb for a moment. Then the rage began. It seemed to rise from the ground, burning the soles of his feet. It traveled through his body, making every molecule vibrate. An outline of fire began encircling him. The Jaquio took a step back. Fear didn't quite fit on his face. It made him look awkward, almost comical.

The Art of the Fire Wheel was working,

but Ryu pulled out his Dragon Sword just the same. He ran toward the Jaquio, letting out a cry that blotted out all sound in the Temple.

With a thrust of the sword, with a swelling of flames, the Jaquio collapsed in a shrieking, bubbling mass of protoplasm. In an instant, he disappeared.

Ryu fell to his knees. Naked anger still coursed through him. The victory wasn't enough; it never would be enough.

"Ryu."

He whipped around. Could it be?

"Ryu, come closer."

His father was alive. Hope flooded through Ryu's body. He ran to his father. Gently, he knelt down and cradled him in his arms. "Are you . . . all right, Dad?"

Dr. Hayabusa shook his head. His face was tight with pain. "Ryu, you must tell me. Who has the statues?"

The statues! Ryu had almost forgotten about them. "The Jaquio has them — *had* them!" he said. "But he's gone! There may not be enough time to find them!"

HHHHHHHHRRRRRROMMMM!

The noise shook the ground like an earthquake. It lifted Ryu and his father and tossed them several feet away. Dr. Hayabusa cried out in agony.

"What's that?" Ryu said.

"It's . . . the Demon, Ryu!" Dr. Hayabusa

replied, fighting to get the words out through his pain. "It's too late to get the statues! We'll . . . we'll have to fight it ourselves!"

Ryu gave his father a sharp look. "Not *we*, Dad. You're in no condition to move."

Dr. Hayabusa tried to rise to his feet. He winced and collapsed. "Paralysis," he said. "You're right, son. I'm not longer for this world. You must go through the narrow crevice at the end of the hall. If you make it through, you'll be in the Demon's lair. Go now. My spirit will be with you."

"I'll be back to get you, Dad. That's a promise."

Ryu bolted out of the room and down the hall. He found the crevice and tried to squeeze through. In the centuries since the Demon had gone to sleep, the earth had shifted, making the entrance only inches wide. Layers of dust and cobwebs peeled off the walls and clung to Ryu's uniform. As he got closer, the heat from within blasted him.

He hoped he was prepared. A Ninja was equipped to survive, but a Ninja was still mortal. Even the great Shinobi had not been able to defeat the Demon.

But Ryu couldn't think about that. The future of the world lay in the balance, and it was up to him alone to do what no one else could.

He had to squeeze himself through the last few feet. When he did, he crouched beside the narrow hole through which he'd come. All he could do for a few moments was stare in awe. He had never seen anything like the Demon.

Next to it, a tyrannosaurus would look petite. Its body was a conglomeration of flesh, bone, and slime, rolling over each other, sputtering and spitting fire. When it moved, it sent hot air currents across the room like jet streams. Its breath sounded like chain saws.

In a corner of the chamber, Ryu saw the Light and Dark statues. They stood together, between two stone pillars that vaulted upward to a high, peaked ceiling. And with each breath of the Demon, they drew closer together, pulsating with light. They were fusing, and Ryu was too late to stop them.

All it took was that first look, and Ryu realized the sad, shocking truth. There was no way on Earth he stood a chance.

CHAPTER 23

HHHHHHRRRRROMMMMMMM!

The Demon shifted its weight. The entire chamber vibrated. Ryu lost his balance and fell.

The Demon's body had moved around a bit, the flesh had slid and churned. There was no easy way to tell the front from the back. Ryu guessed that the Demon had stood up.

He inched closer, holding out his sword. The Demon shifted again. It was turning. Now Ryu could make out its four leg stumps. A large, bulbous growth on its opposite side must have been its head.

They weren't face-to-face yet, but fighting fair was the last thing on Ryu's mind. He charged.

The Dragon Sword sank into the Demon's hide. A slow _hiss_ sounded, releasing a hideous gas.

Ryu pulled out the sword and stepped back. The Demon kept turning. It was as if the stab were a mosquito bite.

Now the Demon was approaching. Its

legs shuffled along the ground, wobbly under the immense weight. Its head lolled from side to side, extending from a thick neck. In the center of its face, a black hole opened up. It had to be a mouth, Ryu realized. It widened to twice its size, looming closer and closer.

Ryu slashed with the Dragon Sword. It passed through the neck.

The Demon's head lopped clean off the body. It fell to the ground with a repulsive *splaaat*. Ryu gasped in horror.

Where the head had been, a gaping hole remained. A hole much larger than the mouth, much more frightening. But Ryu felt nothing but relief. Somehow, he had succeeded where Shinobi had failed. The Demon was dead.

Resting his sword on the ground, he waited for it to fall.

It staggered forward. Ryu figured it was like a chicken with its head cut off, running a few extra steps on nervous energy alone.

But a chicken didn't breathe fire from the hole in its neck. And it didn't keep charging forward as if it could see.

Ryu ran around to the other side of the chamber. The Demon followed. It was still alive.

And it was angry.

CHAPTER 24

Now the Demon was moving faster. It came after Ryu, its bulky body swinging as it walked.

Ryu edged away. He stared at the Demon, afraid to lose eye contact. With his left hand, he felt along the wall.

Until he hit the corner.

The Demon's hole opened wider. Ryu looked around for an escape path. Suddenly flames exploded from the Demon's hole, like the exhaust of a spaceship taking off. Ryu threw himself to the ground. The explosion tore a hole in the wall, clear to the hallway.

Ryu rolled in the only direction he could — toward the Demon. He thrust the Dragon Sword blindly, running it through the underside of the Demon. Each time, a gash opened up, spitting fire and gas. Each time, the gash closed by itself.

The Demon was healing itself instantly.

Ryu rolled to the opposite end of the chamber. Concentrating with all his power, he activated the Art of the Fire Wheel. Flames gathered around him. He whirled his arms, tossing three fireballs toward the headless Demon.

The creature staggered. Ryu watched his ammunition become absorbed into the creature's skin. They had not the slightest effect.

Or had they? The Demon was moving differently. It seemed to be collapsing of its own weight.

It also seemed to be shrinking. The boiling mass of flesh was folding into itself.

Then, almost instantly, the creature began swelling again. It was pulsing with the rhythm of the statues.

"So *that's* it," Ryu said under his breath. The Demon was receiving its energy from the joined statues. If it were left alone, it would take the energy and grow to full strength.

But Ryu was doing exactly what it didn't want. He was weakening it slowly, not letting it collect all its power. Each of his thrusts, each fireball, was keeping the Demon from becoming all-powerful.

Ryu ran toward it, full-tilt. He made rapid thrusts with the Dragon Sword. The Demon spat fire. The fire enveloped Ryu's entire body.

But the Art of the Fire Wheel was protecting him, using the Demon's flame to become stronger.

Now Ryu lunged furiously. With one hand, he plunged the Dragon Sword again and again. With the other, he flung fireballs.

WWWWHHHOMMMMMMMMM!

The Demon had lost control of its legs. It fell to the ground. Behind it, the statues were vibrating wildly. They glowed with garish light now, crashing into each other, out of control. Pieces of stalactites began to fall from the ceiling. Large cracks opened up in the walls.

The place was going to blow. Ryu had to get out. He flew toward his nemesis, slashing.

With a last, pathetic groan, the Demon crumbled to the ground. Its skin began bubbling furiously, rushing inward to a central point. Ryu felt himself being sucked toward it. The floor began to buckle. The left wall caved in, and chunks of marble hurtled toward the disappearing Demon.

It was like a black hole, imploding into itself, sucking in matter and light. Parts of the ceiling fell, exposing the open sky.

Hard as Ryu tried, he couldn't keep from sliding toward the center of the collapsing chamber!

CHAPTER 25

Ryu made one last thrust with the Dragon Sword — downward, into the ground.

It held fast. He dragged himself forward, digging his hand into the gash the sword had made. Holding himself steady with that hand, he used the other hand to remove the sword and plunge it farther away.

Thrust by thrust, Ryu made his way to the edge of the chamber, where the wall had blown in. The farther he got, the weaker the Demon's pull.

By the time he reached the hallway, he could stand up. He sheathed the Dragon Sword and ran back to his father.

Ken Hayabusa lay in a heap just inside the door. "Dad!" Ryu cried out. "I got it! I got the Demon!"

Dr. Hayabusa's eyes fluttered open. "I know, my son. Nothing else could have created the noise around us." He gave a weak smile. "I'm . . . I'm proud of you."

Ryu knelt down and began to hook his

arms underneath his father. "Come on, we have to go!"

"No!" came Dr. Hayabusa's sharp retort. "If you try to save me, we'll both die! When the Demon goes, it will take the Temple with it — and it won't take long. Go now, Ryu! Save yourself!"

"We can do it, Dad!" Ryu protested. "I won't — "

"Look out!" Dr. Hayabusa shouted.

Ryu looked up. An enormous wooden beam was falling from the ceiling. He jumped out of the way, pulling his father with him.

"Ryu, if you wait another second, it'll be too late. Go!"

Ryu hesitated. His father was right — but he couldn't obey him. He could never leave him to die like this. It would be far better for the two of them to die together, united at last.

"Think of your mother, Ryu!" Dr. Hayabusa insisted, as if he were reading his son's mind. "If she loses us both, then the family is ended. She will be alone."

A boulder crashed to the ground inches from Ryu. The force knocked him down.

"GO!" his father repeated. "I will not rest easy unless my son and my wife are alive!"

Ryu made his decision. He got to his feet. "I . . . I will always think of you, Dad," he said. His face was streaked with tears.

Then he turned on his heels and ran out.

The black stone path was blocked. He headed in the other direction, and found a narrow corridor. There were rooms to either side. Some of their doors were open, and Ryu could see test tubes, massive computers, and vats of molted liquid. All bubbling or short-circuiting. All on the verge of destruction.

What sinister experiments was the Jaquio conducting here? Perhaps the world would never know.

He sprinted down the corridor, unable to shake the thought of his father, writhing in the other room. At each step, he wanted to turn back. But he knew the greatest honor he could give his dad was to obey his dying wish.

"Help!"

The voice made Ryu stop. It was coming from behind a closed door at the end of the corridor. As he passed it, Ryu flung it open.

There, sitting tied to a chair, was the red-haired CIA agent. A robot guard was jittering uncontrollably nearby, crashing into a table of electronic equipment.

Ryu rushed in and untied her. At least

there was *one* life he could save. "Come on!" he commanded.

Together they raced through the Temple. There was no easy route — whatever corridor was unblocked, they took.

All around them, the Temple was falling apart. They were running blindly now. For all they knew, they might have been going in circles.

As Ryu's legs pounded the ground, one thought repeated itself in his head: The world was safe again. In seconds he'd be dead, but the world was safe.

GAME HINT

To get through the cliff scene on 5–2, jump onto the cliff as high as you can, using the wall climb technique. Once you've waited for the bird to pass by, then repeat the technique again, and you'll fall to the platform below.

CHAPTER 26

The sky was ablaze. To the east of the Temple, the sun was plump and golden as it rose above the horizon. The scorched soil of the plain began cracking in new places, as it did every morning. The jungle heated up like a steam bath.

But this morning was different from all the others. The living creatures knew. Birds skittered across the sky, confused. The jungle animals remained huddled in their dens, afraid to come out. The ground, which had never moved in centuries, was shifting. The earth was heaving.

Ryu Hayabusa stood on a mound near the edge of the jungle, half a mile from the Temple. Next to him was the red-haired girl. Moments earlier, they had escaped through an underground exit. Now they stared silently, struggling to keep their balance.

Their eyes were fixed on the enormous rock mesa. For thousands of years, it had stood proudly at the same spot. Who knew how long it had been a monument to the

Demon? Who knew where the Demon had come from, why it was here?

Perhaps those question would never be answered. The Temple was sinking. It teetered to one side, then the next, slowly settling into the ground.

The two of them were so intent, they almost didn't notice the darkness coming over the plain.

It was almost pitch-dark before Ryu looked to the rising sun. Its round shape was slowly being blotted out by a shadowy circle.

"It's a solar eclipse!" the young woman said in awe.

"The time of the Dark Moon," Ryu whispered.

"What?"

"'The Demon will begin to wake at the time of the Dark Moon,'" Ryu said. "That's what the inscription said. I guess this is what it meant."

As the moon passed in front of the sun, the area plunged into darkness.

A sonic *boom* rocked the ground beneath them. Ryu and the young woman fell. A cloud of dust covered them. They shielded their faces, coughing uncontrollably.

Ryu could feel light beginning to seep in through his closed eyelids. He stayed huddled to the ground until the dust had settled. Then he opened his eyes.

The sun was full again. It shone on a perfectly flat plain. Where the Temple of Darkness had been, there was now a dense cloud of smoke.

"It's over," the girl said, her voice barely above a whisper.

"Yes," Ryu answered sadly.

Another voice suddenly crackled through the air. "Come in, Sea Swallow!"

Ryu spun around to face the girl. The voice was coming from her shirt pocket.

With a look of embarrassment, she took a calculator-sized object from her pocket. "This is Sea Swallow," she answered into it.

"Our satellites have detected an explosion in the area."

"Yes, sir," the girl responded. "The Temple is destroyed."

"Excellent. Congratulations. Did the Hayabusa boy survive?"

The girl looked nervous. "Y-yes, he did, s-sir," she stuttered. "I — "

"We have one more task for you, Sea Swallow, and then you can come home."

"What's that, sir?"

"Take the statues, and kill Hayabusa."

CHAPTER 27

The girl was speechless. Ryu grabbed the communicator out of her hand.

"Hello, Foster," he said icily. "The statues are gone, and I intend to live."

"Who is this?" Foster demanded. "Who?"

"Not who ... Ryu. Are you going to congratulate me, too?"

Silence.

Ryu waited a full minute. He enjoyed imagining Foster squirm.

"Uh, Ryu," Foster finally said, forcing a chuckle, "you realize, of course, I was talking in code — "

"Ah, yes," Ryu replied, "and 'kill Hayabusa' actually means 'bring him home to a ticker-tape parade,' right?"

"Really, Ryu, did you think we would — "

"It's all clear now, Foster. Your men were the thugs who stole the Dark statue from Doctor Wimple all those years ago — that's how you got hold of it. You've wanted the statues all along, and you would stop at nothing to get them — even if it meant killing people!"

"I beg your pardon. These are serious accusations. Our attorneys — "

"I'll get you, Foster," Ryu said, his voice dark with vengeance. "I'll get you for putting your greed ahead of the world's safety. I'll get you for the murder of my father."

"Your father? What did we have to do with — "

"If I had been able to do it my way, I would have saved him!" Ryu shot back. "You forced everyone's hand, Foster."

"Sea Swallow!" Foster shouted. "I command you to obey me!"

Ryu's eyes locked with Sea Swallow's. They stood that way for a moment, letting Foster bellow.

Finally, Sea Swallow took the communicator. "Foster," she said, "get lost."

With that, she hurled the small instrument into the dusty air.

Together they watched the cloud billow where the Temple had stood. It looked as though it would never settle.

Ryu's mission had been a success. The world was safe. Ryu had faithfully followed his father's letter, had even fulfilled his dying request. He knew he should have been happy for those few moments with his dad, moments he had never expected to see.

But all Ryu would ever remember was that he had left his father in the rubble. Left him to die. He would never forgive himself.

Maybe if his father really had died those many years ago, it would have been better. Maybe he wouldn't feel so torn apart right now.

Ryu felt Sea Swallow's arm come to rest on his shoulder. He wasn't sure he trusted her, but the gesture felt good.

He sighed. For a few minutes, his mind went blank. He thought he saw a figure coming toward them across the plain. A wandering animal perhaps, confused and homeless.

Finally he turned and asked, "What's your name, anyway?"

"Irene," she said. "It's the Greek word for *peace*, you know."

"Irene," Ryu repeated. He looked back to the plain. How ironic, he thought. He finally had reached a kind of peace in his life. He finally had proven worthy of his Ninja training.

But the cost was great. He would live forever with sadness.

"Hey! Can I join the picnic?"

Ryu froze. He was hallucinating, hearing his dad's voice.

"Come on! Help me up!"

Irene was staring over Ryu's shoulder.

Her eyes were wide. "Turn around, Ryu," she said.

Ryu looked down the hill. There was a man struggling to climb up.

Ken Hayabusa.

Ryu rubbed his eyes. When he finished, his father was still there. Smiling. Standing lopsided. One of his legs had a two-by-four strapped to it with a belt.

"Dad!" Ryu cried out. "How — ?"

Dr. Hayabusa shrugged. "The paralysis was temporary. The wood fell into my hands. It was a winning combination. Besides," he added with a wink, "you're not the only Ninja around here."

With a whoop of triumph that carried across the plain, Ryu raced down to his father.

Dr. Hayabusa reared back his head and howled with delight. Atop the hill, Irene was crying.

The Hayabusa family was complete again. For Ryu, a new life had begun.

Two new lives.

Dear Reader,

I hope you liked reading *Ninja Gaiden*. Here is a list of some other books that I thought you might like:

Banner in the Sky
by James Ullman

The Count of Monte Cristo
by Alexandre Dumas

The Karate Kid
by B.B. Hiller

My Side of the Mountain
by Jean Craighead George

The Scarlet Pimpernel
by Emmuska Orczy

The Thirty-Nine Steps
by John Buchan

You can find these books at your local library or bookstore. Ask your teacher or librarian for other books you might enjoy.

Best wishes,

F.X. Nine

Enter the

WORLDS OF POWER™

GIVEAWAY!

WIN A NINTENDO® GAME BOY™ COMPACT VIDEO GAME SYSTEM!

You'll *score big* if your entry is picked in this awesome drawing! Just look what you could win:

GRAND PRIZE: | SECOND PRIZE:

10 Grand Prize winners!

A Nintendo® GAME BOY™ compact video game system

A cool video game carrying case

25 Second Prize winners!

Rules: Entries must be postmarked by November 5, 1990. Winners will be picked at random and notified by mail. No purchase necessary. Void where prohibited. Taxes on prizes are the responsibility of the winners and their immediate families. Employees of Scholastic Inc; its agencies, affiliates, subsidiaries; and their immediate families not eligible. For a complete list of winners, send a self-addressed, stamped envelope to Worlds of Power Giveaway, Contest Winners List, at the address provided below.

Fill in the coupon below or write the information on a 3" x 5" piece of paper and mail to: **WORLDS OF POWER GIVEAWAY**, Scholastic Inc., P.O. Box 742, 730 Broadway, New York, NY 10003. Entries must be postmarked by November 5, 1990. (Canadian residents, mail entries to: Iris Ferguson, Scholastic Inc., 123 Newkirk Road, Richmond Hill, Ontario, Canada L4C365.)

Nintendo® is a registered trademark of Nintendo of America Inc. Game Boy™ is a trademark of Nintendo of America Inc. **WORLDS OF POWER** ™ Books are not authorized, sponsored or endorsed by Nintendo of America.

- -

<u>Worlds of Power</u> Giveaway

Name_____Age_____

Street_____

City_____State_____Zip_____

Where did you buy this <u>Worlds of Power</u> book?

☐ Bookstore   ☐ Video Store   ☐ Discount Store   ☐ Book Club

☐ Book Fair   ☐ Other_____(specify)   WOP190